# Evie Brooks in

# Central Park

## Showdown

SHEILA AGNEW was born in New York and grew up in Dublin with her sister and two brothers. They liked to pretend to be the children in *The Lion, The Witch and The Wardrobe*.

Although Sheila couldn't quite make it to Narnia, she set out to experience what she could of this world. After graduating from UCD, she practised as a lawyer in London, Sydney and New York and got to work in such far-flung places as Accra, Cairo and Bratislava.

Sheila has wanted to be a writer since she was seven and fell in love with *Danny, the Champion of the World*. In 2002, she took time-out from her legal career to write and to travel around Asia. In 2011, she moved to Argentina to learn Spanish and work on a horse farm. The following year, she relocated to Dingle in County Kerry where she wrote the first book about Evie, *Evie Brooks is Marooned in Manhattan*. Sheila based the character of 'Ben' on her own black-and-white spaniel of dubious lineage.

Sheila now lives and writes in New York City.

## DEDICATION

To my parents,

Gerry and Nora Agnew,

with love

## ACKNOWLEDGEMENTS

I am deeply saddened by the loss of my brilliant editor, Mary Webb.

Mary had that rare combination of passion and pragmatism; she

was tough when she needed to be and took very little notice of my

nonsense – thank God! Mary had a wonderful, dry sense of humour. It

was she who brought Evie and Scott to life. She will be much missed.

I am also very grateful to Helen Carr for completing the editing of this

book with such diligence, dedication and can-do spirit.

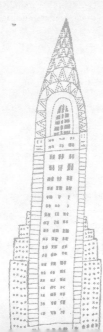

# Chapter 1

I started school today. So did the stye on my eye. I went to bed with two normal eyes and woke up this morning with an ugly reddish-yellowish lump protruding over my left eyelid. Kylie, my best friend here in New York, dropped by before breakfast. Once she had recovered from the shock of the grossness factor (that took about twenty minutes), she set about finding a solution. I rejected her *eye-patches can be cute* suggestion straight away. Ultimately, she dabbed some make-up on me to try to disguise the monstrosity. Putting her hand on my shoulder, she marched me to the mirror to inspect the results and announced, 'See! It looks like a teeny pimple now.'

I think she convinced me because I was *very, very* willing to be convinced. When we went into the kitchen for breakfast, the first thing my uncle Scott said was, 'Is your school uniform skirt supposed to be that short?'

And the second was, 'Is that a stye on your eye?'

I nodded glumly.

'You wouldn't even notice the stye,' Scott said.

Yeah, right! I didn't dignify that with an answer. I bet Scott has never had a stye. He's the kind of person who always looks perfect, even when he's a mess. I look like I can't even spell *perfect* and the horrible boil on my eye made me feel as if I'd been inducted into the *Untouchable* caste in Indian society. My major-league-important, very first day at a new school would be devoted to assuring my classmates that they won't catch anything if they breathe in the same room as me. I knew I was over-reacting, but that didn't stop me from doing it.

My school skirt *is* freakishly short, about half the size of my Irish school uniform skirt. This new skirt doesn't do a lot for my baby-giraffe-type legs. Kylie reassured Scott that soon it will be like totally automatic for me to hold down my skirt on windy days. That seemed to faze him a bit. Kylie is one of only two people who can do that to him. The other is Virpi, his chain-smoking Finnish bookkeeper with a sick sense of humour. At least she has a sense of humour.

Scott obviously couldn't think of anything to say in response to the windy days comment so he busied himself with toasting pop-tarts, which I was too nervous to eat. I nibbled them around the edges like a picky mouse. It's not every day you start school in Manhattan. I'd been so ecstatic when I landed a place at St Sebastian's, the same school that Kylie and my second-best friend in New York, Greg, attend. Before I came to New York and met Greg, I'd never had a real friend who was a boy before, although I don't think of him as a boy. He's just who he is – Greg. I always think of his older brother, Finn, as 'Boy' with a capital 'B', but I wouldn't exactly consider Finn to be my *friend*. He's not my enemy either. He's … never mind. I had enough going on with starting a new school without having Finn occupy lots of space in my head. From the second I opened my eyes (or rather the eye I could open) this morning, I had an uncomfortable, semi-sour feeling in my gut, like facing an exam you are so unprepared for, you can't remember which subject is being tested.

Ben, Scott's dog, whimpered in protest as we left the apartment without him. I made a big fuss about scratching his floppy ears (even though they smell a little ripe right now) because he didn't take any notice at all of my stye, which is more than I can say for Scott. Animals aren't bothered about the way you look.

St Sebastian's is a sprawling, red brick building on West 87th Street. Most of the kids walk or arrive by bus. A handful are dropped off in those sleek, black Lincoln cars that are so common in New York, the ones with the private drivers. There are three nail salons and a glove store across the street from the school. Kylie and I arrived a little early so we hung out in the glove store for a while. Seriously, the only items the store sells are gloves. You can't buy a scarf or a hat or even mittens. Sitting in the display window was a solitary pair of wrist-length red lace fingerless gloves worn by alabaster-white fake hands, clasped together as if in prayer. They can be yours for two hundred and seventy-nine dollars. That's the 'sale' price. Kylie told me she could make an identical pair for a couple of dollars in about twenty minutes. I'm sure she could. She's very talented at crafts, and, at being confident.

Greg met us at the black railings near the school entrance. He looked different in his school uniform; more grown-up, but bizarrely he also seemed shorter. He didn't mention my stye, but I caught him sneaking glances at it. Twice. I felt relieved that his brother, Finn, has finished middle school so at least, I didn't have to worry about bumping into him in my current condition. It's not that I dislike Finn. He just doesn't bring out the best in me, or even the average.

Greg and Kylie steered me through the many corridors (which Americans call hallways) to deposit me in a large room marked J101 for something called '*Orientation for New Students.*' There was a ring of bright-yellow, plastic chairs set in a circle with about fifteen other newcomers sitting on them. They watched me cross the circle to the only empty chair on the far side of the room because they had nothing better to do. First days are awful. At least I didn't trip and fall flat on my face in my short skirt.

The kid beside me, on my right, said 'hi' straight away. His name is Lorcan and, by a big coincidence, he's Irish as well. He talked A LOT, but in a good, interesting way. He is tall and lanky with light green eyes and brown longish hair, styled so that it sticks out stiffly to the left like a wave on the cusp of breaking. You need confidence to pull off that kind of hairstyle and luckily for Lorcan, he seems to have heaps of it. His nose is a little long, giving him a faint birdlike appearance, but not a bird like a hawk, more like a sparrow. I was impressed when he told me he's already thirteen. I have nearly five months to go. Lorcan said that I could probably pass for fifteen on a dark night.

While I was wondering exactly how dark a night he meant, a teacher, a young woman with the blackest of black hair, dressed like a chef in an uber-cool restaurant bounced into the room and I mean 'bounced.' Waves of enthusiasm radiated from her, feeding off every scrap of energy in the room, leaving us all feeling lethargic. Her perfume smelled like half-baked oatmeal raisin cookies with a faint whiff of petrol. Miss Solis told us she had moved to Queens from the Philippines when she was ten years old so she understood *exactly* what it was like to be a newbie, like all of us. We stared blankly at her and a couple of the girls giggled – in a nervous, not a mean way. Miss Solis proceeded to tell us a bit about the school and what we could expect, that kind of thing. She smiled a lot, opening her mouth very widely so we could see her multiple greyish fillings. I have racked up three fillings myself, my mum made sure the dentist put in the white ones.

Every so often, Miss Solis asked, 'Are you with me guys?' and answered herself, 'great, great.' I think she might be a trainee teacher. She had a clipboard with all of our names listed on it and called on each of us to introduce ourselves to the group and describe our families. A girl with gloriously glossy black skin called Nectar went first. (That really is her name). When it was Lorcan's turn, he said that he has two dads who own a software development company and they all moved here a few weeks ago, from Galway, a city in the west of Ireland. Before that, they lived in Hong Kong. I couldn't help feeling a teeny bit envious of Lorcan. It must be sooth-ing to have such a relatively straightforward *normal* family situation. I was dreading my turn so much that my palms got all sweaty. That's not completely accurate, only my left hand got sweaty, which is weird. Anyway, I didn't have a clue what was I supposed to say. I could try:

'Hi, I'm Evie. My mum, who was a brilliant actress (but not rich or famous) died five months ago. I've never had a dad because he ran away before I was born but some guy claiming to be my father turned up at my uncle's veterinary clinic last week. Oh, and this thing that looks like a pimple on my eye is just a stye – it's temporary and it's not conta-gious, in case you were wondering.'

Miss Solis would probably send for the school nurse who would have me popping junior Prozac before lunchtime. So, in the end, when it came to my turn, I just said,

'Hi, my name is Evie. I'm from Ireland and I live with my uncle, Scott, a vet, here in Manhattan now and the rest of my family situation is a bit complicated so I'll explain it another time.'

Everyone stared at me as if I was a weirdo. I felt flustered so I tried to fix things.

'Em, it's not *that* complicated; I'm not saying that my family are part of an international drug cartel or terrorists. Well, I suppose, technically, my father *could* be an international ter-rorist, but I think that must be highly, highly unlikely …'

At that point, Miss Solis swiftly intervened saying,

'Ok, Stevie, thank you for sharing, let's move on now and hear from the next student,' and consulting her clipboard for the next student's name, she said a little faintly, 'Mohammed al Sarwat.'

My day went all downhill from there – so far downhill that waking up with a stye didn't seem like a big deal.

I was hugely relieved to meet Kylie and Greg for lunch in the school cafeteria. I was less than thrilled when Kylie said,

'Guys, have you heard? Apparently there's some new kid from Iceland whose father is in Guantanamo for planning a terrorist attack on the Statue of Liberty.'

'Yeah, I heard about it, the guy's called Steve,' said Greg eating a leafy salad (I still find it bizarre to see kids *choosing* to eat salad).

'Did you meet the new kid in your orientation, Evie?' Greg asked.

I put my cranberry juice down carefully on my tray, feeling somewhat panicked.

'No,' I gulped, 'I think there's some terrible misunderstanding going on.'

Glancing around the cafeteria, it seemed like half the school was whispering about the new weird Icelandic student with terrorist connections. I spotted Camille, who is *not* one of my best friends in New York or anywhere else, pointing at me and whispering to a whole table of kids. Most of them turned and looked at me as if I had head lice. I felt like flinging my fork at Camille's snubby little nose, but I've been in trouble at a school before for throwing metal objects so I ignored her. I don't think she noticed.

Kylie said that Camille was sitting at the table where all the ultra-rich kids sat, the ones who go to the same tennis camps and the same ski schools and whose parents had houses in the right part of the Hamptons and went sailing on their yachts off the coast of Sardinia.

I asked if there were also special tables for the sporty types and the brainiacs and the Glee Club, that kind of thing but Greg shook his head and laughed at me and said that those kinds of cliques only exist in schools on TV and he'd never even *heard* of the term 'Glee Club,' until he saw the TV show.

'In real-life Manhattan, you have your two basic categories – the top one percenters and everyone else,' he explained.

Greg sounded like Dr Winters, his cynical psychiatrist father and nothing at all like Angela, his kinda out-there, theatre-director mom. Finn and Greg shuttle between their divorced parents: 'A' weeks uptown with their dad and 'B' weeks downtown with their mom. I glanced over at Camille's table. I felt a bit sorry for the one percenters; it's much more fun to be with everyone else – and lucky for me I have ready-made school friends in Greg and Kylie, not like the other newbies. The bell rang signaling the end of lunch. I sighed. Three more hours to survive.

# Chapter 2

Straight after school, I went to meet Scott at the Central Park Zoo. He's been appointed as a consultant veterinary there. Today was his first day. He got a call to visit a sick red panda. Normally, I would be excited about a chance to visit the Central Park Zoo. It's one of my *joy-to-the-world sha la la la* places, but I was not in stellar form today. 'Stellar' was last Tuesday's word-of-the-day on Merriam Webster so I'm glad I finally found the opportunity to use it.

I met Scott in front of the sea lion pool in the middle of the zoo. Some of the younger sea lions were enjoying themselves on the slides splashing around in their pool. I could have watched them all day, every day. If my soul existed outside my body in animal form like in the book, *The Golden Compass*, I think it might be a sea lion. I'm not sure; my daemon hasn't settled yet. Kylie thinks her daemon would be a Bird of Paradise. Greg insists his would be a panther. Privately, Kylie and I think that if anyone had a panther daemon, it would be Greg's brother, Finn. Greg's daemon would probably be a beaver minus the sticking-out teeth. This isn't a put down at all; I love beavers and they are very smart and crea-

15

tive and hardworking just like Greg. If Scott had a daemon, it would be an Arabian thoroughbred horse, but with a hint that there was a mule lurking somewhere in his family tree.

As we watched the sea lions frolic, Scott asked me all about how my first day at school went. He was sympathetic about the Icelandic terrorist connection misunderstanding although he found it very funny at first and told me nobody will remember it in a week's time when they have found something new to gossip about. I made a neutral sound like, 'mmm,' because obviously, Scott's way too old to remember that a week in school life can be the equivalent of an adult decade.

A woman wearing a yellow badge saying, 'Sonia Reis, Deputy Administrative Head Veterinary CPZ' met us by the sea-lion pool. Sonia is about Scott's age, thirty-six and everything about her is extraordinarily skinny. When Scott explained he had brought his niece along because she loves animals, Sonia raised her thin, arched eyebrows just a little, and her pencil lips attempted to smile at me. At least, I think that was supposed to be a smile. She has dark wavy hair and wore tiny pink pearl earrings in the smallest ears I've ever seen on a human being.

We followed Sonia to her extremely tidy windowless office where she explained to Scott all about standard procedures when seeing an animal at the zoo and all the online forms that had to be filled out every time he visits a patient. He has to email a copy to almost everyone in the world: local government, state government, federal government, health authorities, yada yada. Administration isn't Scott's thing. He asked Sonia, 'What about emailing a copy to my Great Aunt Juno currently doing fieldwork on the spitting habits of yaks in Outer Mongolia?'

Sonia looked at him very seriously and furrowing her brow, she said, 'No, she's not on the list.'

Scott said hastily, 'I was just kidding,' and Sonia looked at him as if *he* was a yak from Outer Mongolia. Then she continued to drone on about procedures. The way Sonia speaks is fascinating. She is like the most talented ventriloquist in the world. She speaks whole sentences without opening her mouth except for a teeny gap, not nearly enough to even catch a glimpse of her teeth.

Every time, I thought the paperwork was finally completed, Sonia would pull out another piece and say to Scott, 'sign here.' I have fainted once in my life from an extreme shock and I wondered if I could faint from extreme boredom. Finally, Sonia stood up and told a very long story about how the maintenance guy in her apartment building hasn't fixed her refrigerator yet. I'm being charitable by calling it a 'story' because nothing happened. NOTHING. Eventually, Sonia told Scott he was a very welcome new member of the team at the zoo and she was sorry she didn't have more time for chitchat. Scott said that was no problem at all (really), and at last, we were free to see the sick red panda.

A zookeeper named Stanley came with us. He has a mournful face, large, sad, moon-like eyes and a bald head shaped like a lemon. As we reached the red pandas' enclosure, we heard some excited *yip yipping* sounds. I'd never seen a red panda before or any panda for that matter except for a giant black and white panda from China playing the xylophone on YouTube. Red pandas don't look anything like the giant pandas. They look more like raccoons (with a hint of otter) except they are red and white and much cuter. Most of them were chomping stalks of bamboo and roaming around their enclosure with a kind of waddle because their front legs are shorter than their hind ones. Awee, the sick panda, was small, only weighing about the same as a bag of groceries for a one-parent, one-child family. He had been separated from the others so he was in a little enclosed cage for examination, curled up, with his long shaggy tail covering his face. His fur was red like a fox's and he had white triangular ears. He didn't make any yipping noises or take any interest in us at all. Scott consulted his file,

'Awee has a history of depression,' he said.

'I didn't know animals could get depressed,' I said.

'Red pandas are susceptible to depression because of inbreeding,' Scott explained, 'although we have a lot of zoologists here in the US and around the world doing a great job on implementing the red panda species survival plan. They are trying to stamp out inbreeding and the problems it can cause like depression.'

'Red pandas are sometimes called lesser pandas,' he added.

'Being labeled "lesser" would be enough to depress anyone,' I observed.

At that moment, Stanley startled us by making a series of

eerily-realistic yipping noises. He was completely unselfconscious about it. Awee uncurled his tail and I got a look at his face. His eyes were like two glittering black diamonds and he had a white muzzle. He looked like a soft toy, the super expensive kind from FAO Schwartz. Scott handled him very gently, took some blood for testing and some fecal samples, which is a scientific way of saying poop.

Still yipping, Stan stroked Awee's head. He seemed to like it.

'Right, I'll get back to you with the results as soon as I can,' said Scott.

'Yip,' said Stan.

The visit to the zoo distracted me from my problems, but as Scott and I ambled home through the Park, I felt sick in the very bottom of my guts at the prospect of having to go to school again tomorrow. When I casually mentioned to Scott the potential benefits of home schooling, he burst out laughing in a very irritating way and said I will be '*fine.*' Very helpful.

# Chapter 3

I am lying here on my bed in my overly-girly, pink room counting the minutes until my second day of school will begin. In the corner, staring into space is Ella, a huge, soft toy elephant I got as a gift from a famous actor when I was a kid. Ben is sleeping, lying diagonally across the bed taking up a lot of space and making adorable little soft woofing sounds as if he's hunting squirrels in his dreams. He is lying on his back so his large snowshoe paws are scrabbling around in the air like he's riding a bicycle upside down. His eyes are wide open, which is a little creepy. I would like to shut them with my hand the way they do to dead people on TV, but I've never seen anyone do that to someone alive so I think I'll let it go. What I can't let go of is all the stuff that happened last week. I was able to block it out for a while in my excitement (and terror) about starting a new school. However, the most annoying thing about blocked problems is that they sit there in the dark side of your brain, growing bigger and bigger until finally, there isn't enough space left in your head to think about anything but them.

I wish I could make last week go away, so far away that it's not even a memory. Everything had been almost perfect

– we felt almost like a family. Now, Joanna isn't even *speaking* to Scott and it's all the fault of that man, the one who turned up in the clinic as if he was an ordinary veterinary pharmaceutical salesman and casually announced to Karen, our receptionist, that he's my father. The nerve of that guy! Who does he think he is? Oh. I suppose he thinks he's my father. But still – there should be a law prohibiting people from going around disturbing happy people by claiming to be their relatives.

I am trying to piece together all the events of last week. It's doing a mental jigsaw puzzle when you know some of the pieces might be missing. Janet, my godmother back in Ireland, is always criticising the sort of people she calls glass-half-empty types, which is the worst thing anyone can be other than a cheapskate or a mass murderer. I'm concentrating on the pieces of the puzzle that I do have instead of agonising about what might be missing. It takes a lot more effort to be a glass half-full person. I don't know yet if it's worth it.

Let me see. Oh yeah. I remember being in the examining room in the clinic with Scott and Joanna, the other practice vet, and Dodger, the Great Dane. As I carried the microscope across the room, Karen, our receptionist, came in and told us that there was a man in the waiting room saying he was my father. Then I remember being enveloped in a thick duvet of blurry, inky blackness, a warm kind of darkness and, after that, a falling sensation. It wasn't anything like being on the downward path of a rollercoaster. It was much slower, like the way a person jumps off a building in slow motion in a movie. The next thing I remember, I'm in my own bed in my room and Joanna is hovering over me and telling me to keep still and offering me a glass of grape juice.

'What happened?' I asked.

'You fainted, but you're going to be fine.'

'I FAINTED? Are you sure? I've never fainted before. Where's Scott?'

'He's in the clinic,' Joanna replied.

'Scott is dealing with the ... with the ... situation. Everything is going to be okay. Get some rest,' she added as she walked across the room and closed the blinds on the window.

I didn't want to stay in my room in the semi-darkness while Scott was dealing with a situation all by himself. So I flung back the sheets and tried to jump out of bed but the room started spinning and I felt dizzy. Joanna was back at my side immediately, checking my pulse. Then she pulled up a chair beside my bed and sat down in it and crossed her legs, making it very clear that leaving my room wasn't an option. I must have fallen asleep for a while. Although how I could sleep with a situation going on astounds me but I guess fainting must be pretty tiring.

When I woke up, it was dark outside and Joanna was gone so I brushed my teeth and crept downstairs. Nobody was around but Karen, shutting the clinic for the night. At first, she refused to tell me anything about the situation. But after some over-the-top begging on my part, she relented.

'The man who said he is my father; what did he look like?'

'He was cute,' said Karen, 'and tall, you know, maybe not

that tall, probably average height, with black hair and amazing grey eyes just like ... Whatever, and he sounded ... I don't know, I'm not good at recognising accents, but it wasn't like your brogue, it was South African or maybe Australian. I find it hard to tell the difference.'

'What's his name?' I asked.

'Michael Carey.'

I think I gasped a little at that because that's my father's name. Mum told me although there's a blank on my birth certificate in the space for the father's name because the hospital wouldn't let Mum put his name down without his consent. She couldn't get his permission because he ran off before I was born.

'So, what happened next?' I asked Karen.

'The guy, Michael, said he wanted to see you and that he was your father. Then he sat down on that chair right there, the one with the loose back that I keep nagging Scott to fix.'

I gestured impatiently and Karen, who does not like to be rushed, pointedly took an agonising minute to check for text messages on her cell phone before continuing.

'Michael pretended he was reading one of the doggie magazines, the August issue, the one with the photograph of the Pomeranian dressed up as Lady Gaga on the front, so cute, but I could tell he wasn't really reading. I went into the examining room and told you guys about him and that's when you collapsed. What a commotion! Scott and Joanna bumped their heads together so hard that I was sure they would need brain surgery. The microscope shattered all over the floor. I'm still picking shards of glass out of my hair. And Dodger escaped, knocking over all the cans of cat and dog food. I wanted to stick around the examining room and make sure you were ok, Evie, but Scott told me to go back to the desk in the waiting room.'

I nodded, and waited for her to continue.

'Then Scott came striding in here looking very scary. Menacing. That's the word. Like a mafia hit man except obviously Scott doesn't look Italian, more Swedish mafia type. Do they have the mafia in Sweden?'

'I don't know,' I said, restraining myself with difficulty from adding, 'and I couldn't care less.'

'Go on with what happened,' I urged.

'Michael stood up and held out his hand, but Scott just ignored it and said right upfront, "Who the hell are you and what do you want?"

Michael lowered his hand and said, "You must be Scott. Alicia talked about you all the time. You look so like her. Could we maybe go somewhere where we can talk?"

And Scott looked at him as if he was a nasty virus that had just blown here from a cave in Uganda, the kind of plague that makes you cry blood from your eyeballs and said, "You've got thirty seconds right here, right now."

Michael said something like, "I know it wasn't right to just turn up here unannounced but I didn't know what else to do. I only found out a couple of weeks ago that Alicia died and I just, I don't know, I want to find out what happened to the baby and try to make things right."

"Evie's not a baby, she's nearly thirteen," said Scott and he said it with so much disgust that I almost felt sorry for your dad.'

I felt so weird hearing Karen say; 'my *dad*,' but I asked 'what happened next?'

'Scott told Michael, "You've had your thirty seconds and I'm not interested in hearing more. You abandoned Evie before she was even born. You abandoned Alicia, leaving her alone and terrified and pregnant on the other side of the Atlantic. What kind of man does something like that?"

Michael tried to say something. I couldn't make out what it was but Scott cut him off.

"I don't want to hear your excuses. You abandoned them. Even if you are Evie's biological father, it takes a lot more than biology to be a dad. If I ever see you again, if you try to contact my niece in any way, I will get the police involved and have you thrown in jail and deported. Now, get the hell out of my clinic!"

Michael turned and headed to the door and when he reached the door, he turned back and said,

"I understand how angry you must be. But she is my daughter and I will not give up."

'Evie, I am telling you, I felt like I'd been dropped into the middle of a *Lifetime* movie,' said Karen, shaking her head in wonder.

Not a very good one, I thought.

'What happened next? Did the guy, Michael, leave?' I asked.

'Scott moved towards him and I thought for a few seconds that he was going to hit him, but Michael held up his hand and said, "Calm down mate, I'm going."'

Interesting. I stared hard at Karen.

'What did you and Scott do next?'

'I cleaned up the examining room. It took forever but I'm not looking for any extra pay. These things happen and we all have to pitch in. Scott went upstairs to check on you. How are you feeling anyway?'

'Fine,' I said a little impatiently.

'I'm feeling a little scared of Scott right now,' said Karen, 'I shouldn't have told you any of that stuff. Scott's going to fire me. Kill me and then fire me.'

I gave Karen a quick hug.

'No, he's not, he won't ever find out you told me. And you did the right thing! I have a right to know. I mean, the guy *is* claiming to be my father.'

'Yeah, ok,' said Karen, 'and personally, not that Scott asked for my opinion, but I think he should go after that guy for thirteen years of unpaid child support! That's what I would do! Make the guy suffer in his wallet!'

Karen then launched into some complicated anecdote about her cousin's friend, Lindsey, (or it could have been Mindy), who has been chasing her baby's daddy for unpaid child support across five different states. I tuned out. I needed to think.

# Chapter 4

After talking with Karen, I went upstairs to find Scott. He was just coming in the apartment door, struggling to carry a big pizza, half-plain, half-pepperoni, and two cans of zero coke. Scott acted like it was a normal ordinary day. He clearly didn't want to talk about anything important because as we ate, he kept up a running commentary on every supreme escape-artist animal he has ever treated, right up to Dodger. A stranger listening in might get the impression that all of his patients are mentally disturbed. Scott once had a hamster patient called Gladiator who escaped from the clinic here on the Upper West Side of Manhattan and turned up three months later in a penthouse suite in a hotel in South Beach, Miami, pregnant and dressed in a doll's bikini.

Scott said stuff happens in South Beach.

Carlos, the owner, was thrilled to be reunited with his hamster but when he got her home, he changed her name to Gladys.

Scott never mentioned the *situation*. I couldn't figure out how to bring it up. After we devoured most of the pizza, Scott insisted that I return to my room to *rest*. The very last thing I wanted to do was sleep. Instead, I sneaked down to the clinic and crawled into one of my favourite thinking spots behind the crates for the very large dogs in the back room. I had my phone with me so I thought about texting Kylie or Greg, but I couldn't figure out what to say. 'Had pizza for supper, extra cheesy, and btw my dad's turned up.'

I was still thinking about what to say to them when Joanna came in looking for some flea medication for cats, which was pretty odd at that time of night, but we have some annoying clients like Mrs Rubenstein who think fleas fall within the definition of 'emergency.' Scott followed Joanna into the room and shut the door. I swear I was about to jump up and let them know I was there, but Joanna said to Scott,

'So, what are you going to do about Evie's dad?'

There are probably kids out there who could resist the temptation to eavesdrop in those circumstances. I'm not one of them. I didn't make a sound.

Scott replied, 'Do? What am I going to do? Nothing! There's nothing to be done. Even if this guy is *the* Michael Carey, so what? Turning up here now, after what? Thirteen years! That's way too little, way too late.'

'But,' said Joanna, 'what did he say?'

'Who?' asked Scott in a bored voice.

Joanna raised her eyebrows in an exasperated manner.

'Him! Michael! Evie's dad.'

'Not much. I didn't want to hear his excuses. You think I was going to hang around and offer the guy a beer and tell him what a great guy he is for the way he treated Alicia and

Evie?'

'No, of course not,' said Joanna, 'but I thought you might at least talk to him enough to figure out whether he is Evie's father and if so, what he wants to do about that?'

'You really are Pollyanna living in a Pollyanna world,' said Scott in a fake amazed voice. I winced. That's absolutely the meanest thing I have ever heard him say.

'It was Anne of Green Gables actually,' said Joanna stiffly, referring to the summer job she had as a kid – dressing up as Anne Shirley and posing with tourists – 'And I was thinking about EVIE. Doesn't she have the right to know if this Michael guy is her father and to have a relationship with him?'

'I can't *believe* your attitude, Joanna,' said Scott, 'whose side are you on? You want me to send Evie off to the movies with that loser or I know, why don't I let him take her on a trip to Disneyland?'

'Don't be flippant,' snapped Joanna, 'that's not what I'm suggesting at all. All I'm saying is we need to think about this and talk about it with Evie and maybe hear what Michael has to say.'

'*We* don't need to do anything,' replied Scott, 'this isn't any of your business, Joanna. None of it is your business. Evie is my niece. I am her sole guardian and I know what's best for her.'

Joanna looked like Scott had just whacked her across her kneecaps with a hockey stick. Hard. She screwed up her mouth and bit her lip and looked so horribly wounded that

I had to turn my head away. I stared at the wall behind me, which had a bluish stain in the shape of the outline of an owl. I didn't understand how Scott could have been so very mean to Joanna, like she's not important to us at all. She *is* important to us – to me! Joanna's been amazing to me ever since I moved to New York. I would always pick her for my team, no matter what game we were playing.

'You're right, it's none of my business,' said Joanna in a voice so cold it could have regenerated the melting polar caps.

I heard her open the door.

'You know, Scott,' she said, 'I thought you had finally decided to grow up but you don't have it in you,' and she left.

Although I had excruciating pins and needles, I didn't dare move at all because Scott lingered in the room for aaaaaages. First, he kicked some empty cartons around but one of the boxes was full of cans of dog food and he yelped with pain. Then, he mooched around, doing nothing, just staring at the ceiling. When I reached the point of risking developing gangrene from the lack of blood supply to my legs, Scott left, turning off the light, leaving me alone in the dark with only the outline of an owl for company.

＊ ＊ ＊

Ben wakes up and yawns widely in a satisfied manner, distracting me from my thoughts. It's a relief to see his eyes without that disturbing dead wide-eyed glassy look. I scratch

30

his ears absentmindedly. I know this whole mess with the Michael guy and the horrendous row between Scott and Joanna isn't my fault. Really, I do. I know that one hundred percent absolutely clearly . . . but it *feels* like it's my fault in a roundabout way. So, it's up to me to try and fix things and I'm not feeling overconfident about my abilities as a fixer.

# Chapter 5

Greg and I walked slowly up the nave of the cathedral, about midway in the procession, he carrying his black rabbit, Dr Pepper, and me walking Ben, although sometimes it seemed like he was walking me. Directly ahead of us, a baby camel swayed slightly right and left in a dignified manner, led by his owner, a hefty, middle-aged woman with waist-length, black hair and muscular forearms, decked out in costume like a character in *A Thousand and One Arabian Nights*. A little further ahead, we spotted a kangaroo, a donkey, three ducklings, a small unidentifiable furry animal and a huge Galapagos turtle. Close on our heels were a pot-bellied pig, two pheasants, a fennec fox, a macaw and thousands and thousands of dogs and cats. It looked more like a scene from Noah's Ark in Biblical times than an ordinary Sunday in Manhattan except none of the animals walked in pairs and there wasn't even a hint of rain. We passed Scott, sitting in the fourth pew, and he winked at us.

Every year since 1985, in celebration of St Francis of Assisi, there has been an annual Blessing of the Animals in the Cathedral Church of St John the Divine, an enormous grey Gothic building on Amsterdam Avenue and West 112th

Street. On that day, everyone is welcome to bring his or her pets into the church to be blessed. I haven't been to church a lot in my life but if animals were allowed, I think I would go almost every day. The thing that surprised me most was the silence. With thousands of animals, I thought that it would be bedlam but it was quiet except for the occasional bark or the flap of wings.

As we approached the altar, the procession broke into separate lines towards the priests or the reverends for the individual blessings. Well, I'm not sure exactly who they were but they were men in religious-looking black robes. Greg and I got separated in the crowd and I wound up in a line behind a teenage boy carrying a tiny brown cardboard box not much bigger than a matchbox, with air holes punched into it. Maybe a tiny baby white mouse, I thought, scouting around and standing on my tippy-toes to get a better view. The kid opened the box and the priest shrieked and jumped to the side so quickly that he landed very heavily on my right foot. (I still have a black toenail). Inside the box crawled an enormous, obese cockroach. Barf. The priest recovered his composure pretty quickly and mumbled something about St Francis's love for all God's creatures, big and small, fat and thin, cute and ... not-so-cute. Then he sprinkled a few drops of holy water into the box from a very safe distance. When it was Ben's turn for the blessing, he behaved himself very well, only sneezing twice rather loudly and extending his left paw to the priest for a high five.

The crowd in the cathedral didn't look anything like the

people you see every day in midtown Manhattan. You could tell these people didn't give much thought to their clothes; they wore stretch pants and old grey sweatshirts, which said *Harvard* or *Princeton* or *Google*. They weren't nearly as skinny and busy and important looking as most Manhattanites. I spotted Debbie, who runs an animal sanctuary uptown and I waved at her. She waved back with such enthusiasm that one of the bundle of wriggling kittens in her arms fell to the floor, landing perfectly balanced on its paws like a … cat.

Scott and Greg found me and we took a heap of photos of the animals to show to the kids in school. We walked all the way home and I thought it is funny that I can miss Ireland so much and love New York so much at the same time. And for a short while, I almost forgot about the *Big Freeze* between Scott and Joanna.

It's been nearly a month since the *Big Freeze* began. My clumsy attempts at bringing Scott and Joanna together haven't paid off. To be fair to myself, it's pretty hard to effect a reconciliation between two people if you have to pretend you don't know that they're fighting.

Joanna hardly ever comes up to the apartment anymore. I miss her.

There's a tension in the clinic that was never there before. Sometimes, it's so thick and cloying, I feel I can almost touch it. Scott and Joanna are being ridiculously formal and polite with one another. It's all: 'Could you please pass me the small forceps if it's not too much trouble,' and 'Certainly, I'll do that.' I'm beginning to wonder if that bump on their heads really did affect their brains. I wish Mum were here. She'd instinctively know what to say and do. She was a born peacemaker. Everyone said so. Nobody has ever said that about me.

# Chapter 6

Today was a clear, sunny, early October Saturday, the kind of morning on which it's impossible to maintain a bad mood without a great deal of effort. Scott suggested we take Ben for a long walk over by the East River. We took a taxi to East 34th Street and the FDR Drive and started our walk along a concrete footpath by the choppy, swollen river. We could see the buildings of Brooklyn on the far side.

We were probably the slowest people on the path. Intense-looking joggers dodged around us without breaking their rhythm. We were even overtaken by a motorised wheelchair, driven by a wrinkled old white toothless woman dressed in a blue hospital gown. Scott was clearly preoccupied because he didn't automatically glance at the pretty female joggers with their slicked back ponytails and their focused faces. I noticed that none of them were sweating. Kylie's Mom, Rachel, said a few weeks ago that some women in Manhattan have their sweat glands surgically removed. Joanna replied 'that's an urban myth' or maybe she said, she *hopes* that's an urban myth, I can't remember.

There were few interesting smells for Ben to sniff until we

reached the East River Park where his nose vibrated loudly with excitement. Scott told me that a dog's nose is thousands and thousands of times more sensitive than human noses; we have about 5 million cells devoted to smelling but they have about 220 million.

'Wow,' I said, but then I thought of some of the more unpleasant putrid garbage type smells in the city especially in the summer and I didn't feel envious of Ben. If I could have a superpower-enhanced sense, I would choose sight or maybe hearing, definitely not smell. Scott said that he would choose touch.

A text from Lorcan distracted me.

'Call me ASAP'

I waved Scott and Ben ahead and leaned against the pier to call Lorcan. He invited me to hang out at his apartment around 7ish – just me, nobody else. I felt sort of honoured because Lorcan had very quickly established himself as one of the cool popular kids at school.

'Will your dads be there?' I asked.

'Yeah, of course they'll be here. It's Saturday. It's their laundry night. Nobody who lives in Manhattan goes out on a Saturday night.'

'Um, see you later,' I said thinking that for someone who has only lived in Manhattan for a couple of months, Lorcan had acclimatised very quickly. Finn would never say something like that. It's the kind of smug elitist comment the one percenters would make. Lorcan's been sitting at their lunch table in the school cafeteria a lot so he'd probably picked it up from them.

When I caught up with Scott and told him about my plans with Lorcan, he began to interrogate me, which is so not like him.

'Lorcan's just a new friend,' I pointed out. 'I like being with him. He's Irish. We get to talk about stuff we miss about Ireland like Club Milks.'

'Clubs?' said Scott in an amazed voice, 'you're a long, long way from going clubbing young lady.'

He actually said that – 'young lady.' What has happened to SCOTT? Seriously, I need to dial 311 and get on to the mayor's office. Are they putting something different in the water?

Scott continued to rant.

'I've seen those junior clubs on MTV, where they have the separate VIP area and everything. It's crazy. I know EXACTLY what goes on in those kinds of places. You're not going out with that Lorcan kid tonight.'

'A club milk is a miniature CHOCOLATE bar,' I wailed, 'it's a biscuit – or you'd say a cookie – covered in chocolate … and, and, never mind, Lorcan and I, we're going to hang out in his apartment. His dads will be there! We're just FRIENDS!' I said huffily, thinking Scott sounded way too much like an annoying parent.

'Of course, you're just friends,' said Scott, looking startled, 'you're not even thirteen yet. And BTW, I think thirty would be a good age for you to start exploring romantic relationships. Girls start dating too early.'

'THIRTY! That's ludicrous. Joanna was totally right, you're NOT a grown-up,' I huffed.

Scott stopped walking instantly as if he was a toy robot and I had clicked his switch to the off position. He stared at me in a very disconcerting way, looking extremely serious and grown-up like my math teacher, Mr Papadopoulos.

'Wow, look at that bird, Scott,' I said a little desperately, pointing at a passing gull, 'it's so, em, so … bird-like' I added lamely.

Scott didn't buy that distraction. Nobody above the age of two would have.

'How do you know Joanna said I wasn't a grown-up?' he asked quietly.

'Em, that's not important, I think what *is* important is Joanna is hurt. I think we *are* her business. You know, like, she's one of us.'

Scott ran his hand through his hair so it stood up in spikes, the way he always does when he's agitated.

'You need to say sorry to her,' I added a little forcefully.

'Evie, you're right. I know. Did Joanna tell you about our fight?'

'No,' I said, 'and stop trying to go off topic,' I added (rather brilliantly I thought), 'you need to apologise to Joanna!'

'I will,' he said bleakly.

'When?' I asked.

Scott sighed. 'I feel like I have my very own personal Jiminy Cricket hanging around my neck,' he grumbled.

'When?' I repeated.

'As soon as we get back to the clinic,' he answered and I felt satisfied and thought that perhaps, I'm not such a talentless fixer after all.

Scott said, 'Evie, I've been meaning to talk to you about the day you fainted. I'm sorry I haven't before. It must have been weird for you that we didn't talk about stuff. Let's sit down on this bench.'

'Ok,' I said.

We sat on the bench and I waited for Scott to say something. He didn't appear to be in a hurry. We watched the Circle Line cruise boat go by and I waved at the tourists wearing shorts and sneakers with white socks and baseball caps. Most of them waved back. I got bored with waiting for Scott to say something so I gave him a nudge.

'Has this something to do with the guy who came into the clinic last month saying he was my dad?' I prompted.

Scott seemed grateful to get the help with the starting off bit.

'Yes,' he said, 'I told him to get lost and never come back.'

'Good,' I said.

'Yeeees, but I'm sorry, I should have talked to you first,' Scott said.

'That's ok,' I said.

'Aren't you curious about him?' Scott asked.

I shook my head. 'Nah. Couldn't care less.'

'Not even a little bit curious?' quizzed Scott.

'Nope. When I was little, I often thought about my Dad turning up – what he would say, what I would say, what kind of presents he would bring me, how he and Mum would get married and we'd all go live in some amazing villa on a beach or maybe in Italy with olive trees. We'd be a real family like the kind on TV. But I haven't thought like that for a very long time. What I think about now is Mum lying all yellowish and tired looking in that white hospital bed. It would have meant something to her if he'd turned up, even then. But now! I mean, what's the point? Who cares? Not me!'

Scott patted me awkwardly on my back as if I had hiccups. I continued blabbing on.

'All those years Mum spent waiting for him to get in touch. He never even sent a birthday or a Christmas card, not one lousy card.'

Scott looked at me in a way like he felt bad for me and I rushed to explain,

'It didn't matter. We always got loads of cards from heaps of people. I don't think anyone in the world had as many friends as Mum. We didn't need Michael's stupid cards. We didn't need anything from him. And we don't need him now. I mean, *I* don't need him now. I have you.'

Scott smiled and gave me a hug. I was glad to hide my face in his very soft cotton t-shirt for a few minutes so I could blink back tears of rage.

'I agree with you, Evie. But I need to tell you something. I found out this week that Michael has filed a lawsuit to try and get custody of you. It's nothing for you to worry about. My lawyer says we will easily beat it. The guy has no rights when it comes to you. Not after all this time.'

I felt beyond terrible hearing this, like I was going to throw up for real this time. From my experience with Scott's old sneaky snake-like girlfriend, Leela, I knew lawyers cost a lot of money.

'Don't look like that,' said Scott, hugging me again, 'my friend Rob, you remember, the one with the kid Harry and Zak, the meerkat, he's going to be my lawyer, he's great and he doesn't cost too much. He's just going to write some papers and the Judge will dismiss Michael's case. Throw it out! That's all there is to it.'

'Will we have to be in court?'

'No,' said Scott, 'it's nothing, it's about as serious as a parking ticket case. No big deal. Michael doesn't have a chance.'

'Ok,' I said, 'I'm sorry about all this trouble and the money and the lawyer.'

'You have nothing to be sorry about!' Scott reassured me, 'and I'm not as broke as you seem to think I am! The clinic's doing great and the extra job at the Zoo helps.'

I felt better knowing that we weren't on the brink of bankruptcy. We walked up to the baseball diamonds and sat on some bleachers and watched a team of girls beat a team of guys at softball. It wasn't even close. The girls crucified them.

# Chapter 7

That evening, I went to Lorcan's apartment, a huge ground floor loft in a converted warehouse in Tribeca. It was very cold. Simon, one of Lorcan's dads, let me in and sang out, 'Lorcan, your girlfriend's here.'

It was highly embarrassing. On the other hand, I felt very grown-up being called anybody's 'girlfriend.' Lorcan shouted out that he was in the john and he'd be out in a minute. (Boys can be so weird. I would never in a million years announce to a boy visitor that I was in the loo (unless the visitor was Greg and he doesn't count as a *boy* boy). Simon's from Galway in Ireland, but you would never be able to tell from his accent, which sounded more smoothly and blandly American than most Americans I knew.

Peter (Lorcan's other dad) handed me a pomegranate smoothie and then he and Simon went back to the kitchen area. I looked around me. The walls were hung with enormous blurry photographs of Lorcan and his dads in Hong Kong. I think the pictures were supposed to be out-of-focus.

Lorcan's family was too cool to have much furniture. There was only one chair in the room, which looked like it was made out of barbed wire. I sat down, cross-legged, on an

43

old, raggedy, threadbare rug in the middle of the floor and sipped my smoothie.

Simon stepped back into the room and let rip a roar in the strongest Irish accent imaginable,

'OH MY GOD PETE, SHE'S SITTING ON THE NAZMIYAL!'

He startled me so much that I almost dropped my smoothie. Simon sprinted across the room, grabbed my arms and swung me off the rug as if I were a toddler. He totally robbed me of the tiniest morsel of dignity.

Simon practically had tears in his eyes. I don't think he'll ever forgive me for the heinous crime of sitting on his stupid rug.

Lorcan was very nice and cool about the incident. He said that the rug was hideously ugly and that I shouldn't stress about it. (I wasn't stressed about it. Simon's the one who freaked out about nothing, but it was sweet of Lorcan to try and reassure me). We had fun hanging out. There really isn't any topic that Lorcan can't talk about. He told me that when he was little and lived in Hong Kong, he thought he was Chinese except he just looked different.

'Didn't that tip you off that you *were* different?' I asked.

'No,' said Lorcan, 'there was a kid in my class who always had snots in his nose. I thought I was different in the same kind of trivial – but not disgusting – way.'

Lorcan didn't realise he wasn't Chinese until his amah (that's what he called his nanny) told him. He was devastated.

\* \* \*

That night when Scott came into my room to say goodnight, I asked, 'Well, how did it go with Joanna?'

'I'm not going to lie to you Evie, not so great.'

'What does that mean? Not so great? You said sorry, right? You used the word "sorry"?'

'Yeah, I did. But sorry isn't a magic word. You can't just wave it around like a wand and voila, the rabbit jumps out of the hat into your arms.'

'What are you on about?' I asked, 'Is Joanna supposed to be the bunny in this scenario because I don't think she'd like that at all. I hope you didn't start talking about rabbits jumping out of hats.'

'No, I do have some experience with dealing with women. What do you take me for?' Scott asked.

'Well, that's a relief,' I said, 'what did Joanna say when you said sorry?'

'She said she doesn't want to become my partner in the clinic anymore,' he said bleakly.

'Way harsh,' I said sympathetically, 'do you think she means it?'

'I don't know,' said Scott.

'What else did she say?' I asked.

'Hmm. Something less than flattering about my fitness as a partner. I think her sugar levels might have been a little low. You know what she's like when she hasn't had her daily box of muffin bite bakes *Baked by Melissa*.'

I didn't buy that one little bit. I glared at him.

'I'm not sure you apologised properly, an *all-the-way* on your knees apology, a *I completely messed up and I will die if you don't forgive me* apology.'

Scott looked a little like someone who has brazenly skipped the line at the movie theatre in front of a hundred people but acts like nobody noticed.

'You can't push people, Evie. I said I was sorry, what else can I do? Joanna is Canadian.'

My mouth dropped open. I mean, seriously! Scott's old *Joanna-is-a-Canadian* stand-by.

It seemed pretty obvious to me that Scott didn't do nearly well enough with his apology. Sounded like an 'F' grade apology to me. I was about to tell him so when something stopped me. I felt suddenly older than Scott and wise like Oprah. Scott needed to figure this one out by himself. He looked at me in a puzzled way.

'Don't worry, Evie. Joanna will come around; give it time.'

'Ok,' I said.

After all, I thought, Joanna has a very big heart. I decided to do as Scott suggested and give the *Big Freeze* plenty of time to thaw. I had lots of other distractions like school and Lorcan. And I certainly wasn't going to waste energy thinking about that Michael guy. Scott's lawyer, Rob, would take care of that and make him go away. Michael was nothing but a . . . nothing.

# Chapter 8

So, I gave it time, lots and lots of time, four and a half months to be exact. It's now the third week of February, two weeks after my thirteenth birthday. I thought I'd feel different being a teenager and adults would treat me differently. But I feel like I always have. I haven't noticed the slightest difference between being twelve and thirteen. None at all. Disappointing. But Deirdre and Cate, my best friends back in Dublin, remembered my birthday and sent me lovely presents. So did my godmother, Janet. It was Scott who gave me the most AMAZING present, my very own glossy brown, leather saddle for Luna.

My present from Greg is currently pooping in my closet. His name is Persie (short for Personality Disorder). Greg's dad named him. I haven't seen any evidence of a personality disorder ... or a personality. Kylie says Persie is a *problem present*. Most New Yorkers regard pigeons as rats with wings. I'm not particularly fond of them myself. Greg's doorman, Jorges (the 'J' sounds like an 'H'), gave Persie to Greg as a gift. Since Greg's Dad can't stand pigeons, Greg re-gifted Persie to me for my birthday. Obviously, I didn't go overboard in thanking him.

Persie isn't a clean white pigeon that you might hope to pass off as a large dove. He looks filthy no matter how many baths we give him in the kitchen sink and a whitish sludge drips out of his little backside almost all the time, even when he is eating. I have yet to discover any redeeming qualities. I can't imagine our flamboyantly-dressed Brazilian house-keeper, Eurdes, welcoming Persie with open arms. Her idea of an appropriate welcome would probably involve a sweeping brush and a dustpan. Luckily, there have been so many changes around here in the last few months that Persie has slid past Eurdes's radar undetected so far.

The most unwelcome change has got to be Jeffrey, Joanna's intense new boyfriend with poor posture. Jeffrey's a professional activist. He probably got the stooped shoulders from hoisting heavy placards in thousands of demonstrations. When I first met him, I asked if he was an eco-warrior, but he said that he embraces any cause that speaks to him. He takes himself very seriously. At least someone does.

Kylie thinks that Joanna only acquired a boyfriend to try to make Scott jealous. Obviously, Kylie hasn't met Jeffrey yet.

I'm pleased that the tension between Scott and Joanna has eased off over the last few months. They were almost back to being friends until Holly came along, but that's not Holly's fault. You see, a few weeks ago, Karen announced that she had decided to go back to school part-time to study to become a veterinary nurse. We were all thrilled for her, but we needed to find someone to cover for her on Tuesdays and Thursdays when she's at school. Joanna said she'd take care of it and put an advertisement for a new part-time receptionist in *New York Dog* Magazine. The very next day, a freezing cold Saturday, Holly turned up at the clinic with a large dog she had recently adopted, a Louisiana Catahoula Leopard Dog named Buddy. He doesn't look anything like a leopard except he has black spots. Scott's always appreciates people who adopt dogs who need a home and he was in a jovial super-friendly mood during the check-up. Scott said,

'Buddy. Holly! Good one!' but Holly wrinkled her nose in confusion.

Scott said, 'Like the singer, with the square glasses … *the* Buddy Holly, Buddy Holly and the Crickets … he died in a plane crash,' but Holly still looked confused so Scott said he felt old and he let it drop.

As Scott gave Buddy a check-up, Holly pretty much told us her life story. She's twenty-two years old and grew up in a small town called Dudley in Georgia. There's only one stop sign in the town and no Starbucks. I could listen to Holly talk forever. If candy floss could speak, it would sound like her. (They call it cotton candy here. Greg thinks the name candy floss is dumb – who would want to eat candy dental floss – but Kylie thinks candy floss is a fantastic name because it reminds you to floss after eating it. It wouldn't remind me; I've never flossed in my life).

Holly told us that she moved to New York on the second day in January (she meant to come on New Year's Day, but she missed the bus) to take acting and singing classes because she wants to be a star on Broadway. She found a job as a coat-check girl in a nightclub called *Red* in Nolita but they tried to make her dye her hair red (which she didn't think would suit her skin tone at all) so she quit. She found a waitressing job in a Peruvian restaurant in Soho, which specializes in serving seventeen different kinds of ceviche. Holly said that we could feel real safe eating there any time because nobody spits or pees in the food – even if it is sent back.

'Good to know,' said Scott, 'in the unlikely event I am ever tempted to dine out again.'

Holly started to sniffle. Scott looked alarmed.

'I was only kidding!' he said.

'Oh, I know,' said Holly, searching in her pockets for a non-existent tissue, 'it's not that. I'm upset because I got fired from the restaurant job.'

She explained that the previous night, her ex-boyfriend, a former drug dealer, who has just been released from prison in Alabama, tracked her down to New York and turned up at the Peruvian restaurant and pulled a knife on her boss in a fit of jealousy. He thought (wrongly) that Holly was dating the boss.

Holly's boss called the police and the ex-boyfriend ran off. After the police left, the boss fired Holly as if it was her fault that her crazy knife-wielding ex showed up. So, here she was, jobless and with virtually no friends in New York. Telling the story was traumatic for her. She burst into hysterical tears at the end.

Scott hired her as the new part-time replacement on the spot, even though I was waving my arms frantically at him and mouthing 'noooooooooo' behind Holly's back. It's not that I didn't like Holly, but it wouldn't take a genius to realise that Joanna wasn't going to be impressed.

After Holly left, greatly cheered up by having a new job, Scott turned to me and said that telling Joanna was going to be a 'little tricky.'

I looked at him.

'Joanna's much less likely to have a total flip-out if you're around, so maybe we can tell her together,' he said.

'What?' I said, 'you want to use me, your thirteen-year-old niece as some sort of human shield?'

'I wouldn't express it quite like that but basically, yes,' said Scott.

'No, I won't do it,' I said.

'I'll give you an extra hour a day on the iPad for two weeks,' he offered.

'Make it a month and you have yourself a deal,' I answered.

'Done,' he said.

Joanna's reaction was even worse than I expected. She remained ominously calm, only slightly raising her eyebrows when Scott admitted that Holly had no experience with working with animals or as a receptionist. As Scott tried to explain how he had hired a new employee without so much as consulting her, Joanna kept saying, 'I see,' in a tone that unmistakably indicated that what she meant was, 'I see that you're a total idiot.'

I'm not going to gloss over things. It definitely was a pretty major setback in the road of repairing their relationship. But things have settled down a bit particularly since Holly has turned out to be a very popular receptionist, much adored by many of the patients and their owners – when she's here that is. She has to travel back and forth from her new apartment in Astoria, in Queens, and she's often late.

Holly is quite short and endearingly chubby with a heart-shaped face and big blue eyes. Her hair is the same colour as the original classic blonde Barbie and it is very big and wavy like the pageant contestants on TV. She is extremely fond of wearing waist-length fake fur jackets in a variety of very bright and unusual colours like lilac and hot pink and caterpillar green. They aren't very practical for the cold weather because they are sleeveless. Greg is Holly's biggest fan. He always wants to hang out here on Tuesdays and Thursdays now, even when I am not around! He says it's for research because he's writing a screenplay and the main character is based on Holly. He won't let Kylie or me read any of his screenplay yet. Kylie is annoyed with him because she wants to be the star in his film but he says he can't have an Asian play the *Holly* character, which Kylie says is discrimination of the worst kind. I didn't like to ask her what is the best kind of discrimination. I have some sympathy for Greg. I can't imagine Holly being played by Kylie in a movie. But I have not been brave (or stupid) enough to say this to Kylie. I just make empathy noises like 'mmmm' when she complains about Greg's attitude.

Even Ben has fallen for Holly's charm. He follows her around the clinic with the exact same look on his face as

Greg has – all sloppy, goofy adoration with his tongue hanging out. (It's a better look on Ben). When Holly is working, she always brings Buddy with her. Ben's not happy about that at all. He's used to being the number one dog around here and he must be exhausted from ensuring that Buddy doesn't sneak anything belonging to him. Ben's going to collapse soon. No dog could keep up this kind of vigilance. Greg thinks Ben needs to go to a yoga for dogs class they are holding over on East 64th Street so he can learn to relax. When I raised this suggestion with Joanna, she snorted very loudly. She's been snorting so much lately, I'm a little worried she might be risking damaging the membranes in her nostrils.

Talking of nostrils, I'm certain that Mrs Davidson's nostrils are distorted. She is always sticking her finger in them. She doesn't seem to care if people are looking or not. She doesn't seem to care much about anything. She certainly doesn't care about pretending to teach us. I thought that school in New York was going to be different to Ireland; edgier, more glamorous, more exciting, more everything. But it is basically the EXACT same. There are some brilliant teachers … and then there are the Davidson types and worse. The kids are the same too, some great, some not so great. Lorcan is definitely on the great side. He always has something interesting to say. He hangs out all the time with Kylie and Greg and me. I'm lucky that they like him and welcomed into our gang without any bother. Camille, however, is a pain in the butt. She is always finding ways to put me down. I read somewhere that *nobody can put you down without your consent.* That's the kind of thing that sounds deep and meaningful but is not helpful at all. I'm definitely not giving Camille permission to do anything. She does what she likes and she's popular, so kids listen to her. She's always making up petty little lies about me. It's not like she consults me in advance, so that I can refuse permission! I never find out about the lies until after she's spread them. I ignore her as much as I can, which isn't easy because she's always hanging around Lorcan and inviting him to cool places. Sometimes he says yes.

# Chapter 9

I took part in my first horse riding competition today. It didn't go anything like planned except for my hair, which was perfect, thanks to Kylie's mom, Rachel, who knows how to do Dutch braids. Tamara, Finn's depressingly-sweet girlfriend took part as well, but in a much higher class than me. Her hair was also perfect, but it always is, so it couldn't have been much of a treat for her. Scott couldn't come because he had an emergency, a chipmunk with a broken jaw. But a big bunch came along to support Tamara and me: Kylie, Greg, Finn, Lorcan, Akono and Tamara's slimy twin brother Coltan. When Camille found out that Lorcan was coming, she invited herself along because it has been patently obvious for some time now that she fancies him. He can't stand her. Well, that's what he told me. But I've noticed that it doesn't stop him from saying yes when her daddy gives her cool concert tickets.

The gymkhana took place on Long Island (which, everyone just calls the island, and they always say *out on the island*). We had to go in two cars. Finn wasn't in my car and I was grateful for that because things have a habit of going wrong when he's around. Coltan nearly knocked me down in his haste to get into the same car as Finn. I've never seen him move with so much speed before. Usually he's too cool to be anything other than languid. He even stands like he's leaning against a wall.

Akono rode in the car that I was in even though *he's* Finn's best friend, not Coltan. Akono sat beside Kylie and teased her a lot. She was so able to throw it back at him. I was too nervous about the competition to join in the conversation. My legs shook a little the whole ride, but nobody noticed or at least they were kind enough to pretend not to notice. Danielle, my instructor, and some of the grooms had brought the horses, including Luna, much earlier in the morning. As soon as we arrived, I made straight for Luna's stall and gave her half a bag of baby carrots and whispered to her in soothing nonsense language that only she and I understand. After I had finished grooming her and tacking her up and after a final check that the girth was tight enough and the stirrups the right length, I went into the corner of the ring laid with grainy grey sand, for Danielle's inspection. I passed except she told me to fix my shirt because it was sticking out at the back. My class was first, and I was the oldest in the class, so it was a little embarrassing to be competing with other kids who were mainly eight and nine year olds. But I thought it would be a lot more embarrassing to be beaten by one of them.

Finally, it was my turn to ride around the ring over the little jumps. As soon as I mounted Luna, my nerves disappeared and I felt as excited as if we were about to take part in the Olympics. I wondered if I would be on the Irish or the US Olympic Equestrian team; I could visualise myself staring straight ahead on the winners' podium as the Irish and the US flags were lowered and they played both national anthems as a single tear coursed down my cheek. Danielle called out; 'Evie, focus!' and that snapped me back to real time.

It was a chilly morning and Luna's white breath rose in the air in front of me, mingling with my own exhaled breath. The ground was a little hard and Luna's hooves made a satisfying solid thumpety-thump sound as we cleared the jumps. At the very last jump, as we sailed over, the saddle slipped violently to the left. I tried to grab Luna's mane but shot clear over her head and landed on the ground with such force that I thought every bone in my body had broken into a million pieces. I couldn't breathe. So many people crowded around me, sounding very far away and far too close at the same time and someone kept asking me questions, like, 'What's your name?' and 'Can you move your head?' and at the same time, someone else was saying, 'Don't try to speak,' 'Don't move your head.'

'I'm suffocating,' I gasped.

'Give her some space,' someone said.

Then I felt someone pick me up and carry me out of the ring. I said 'hi' and Finn said 'hi, you' back.

'Put me down,' I said, and tried to put some force into my voice but he ignored me, which I didn't actually mind because it felt very special to be carried by Finn. Although,

I have to say that it wasn't like the movies at all. Finn carried me like I was part of his hockey equipment. A thick strand of my hair had loosened from my braids and got in his mouth and he had to spit it out. The nicest part was how very close his face was to mine. I felt a little like Bella in the *Twilight* books always getting rescued by Edward except he fell in love with her because of her smell and I'd definitely prefer if someone liked me for some other qualities. Anyway, I didn't smell so good. I think I might have landed in some horse poop.

Finn put me down very gently on a bench right outside under an archway. Danielle came rushing out followed by the whole gang. She yelled at Finn, 'You shouldn't have moved her, that was dangerous,'

I said, 'I'm fine thanks to him. I couldn't breathe in there.'

Danielle said she had to call Scott. I begged her not to but she said she had to. Scott asked to speak to me and said, 'Hang in there Black Beauty,' and he told me that the chipmunk was going to be fine, probably better than me and that he was already on his way out to get me. I felt bad I had caused so much trouble.

Danielle said that I had learned a very important lesson about tightening the girth on my saddle.

'But I did tighten it,' I protested.

'It wouldn't have loosened to that extent if you had done it properly,' she replied.

'But I did,' I said again and she sighed and said,

'Evie, I know you're not lying, I know you believe what

you are saying but you slip off sometimes into your own daydream world and you think you've done something but really you were just, you know, out there, losing time.'

The injustice rankled.

'I know I drift off sometimes, but I DID tighten the girth properly,' I muttered.

'We'll talk about it again another time, when you have recovered from the shock,' Danielle said.

'If Evie says she tightened the girth, then she did it,' said Finn in his low voice.

That surprised me. Whenever I think I've started to understand Finn, he says something that makes me realise I don't have a clue.

From inside the arena came the sound of one of the organizers announcing over the loudspeaker that the 'little girl' who had taken a fall was ok and that the competition was about to resume. So much for being thirteen.

'I have to go back in and watch Tamara,' Finn said to me, 'you're ok?'

I nodded. 'Thanks,' I said.

He smiled his lopsided half-smile at me and tucked some of the loose strands of my hair behind my left ear before strolling off. I felt a little dizzy. Well, it had been a heck of a fall.

When I felt steady on my legs again, Greg, Kylie and Lorcan came with me around to the stalls behind the arena to check on Luna and give her some hay. She was fine and looked very pleased to see me. Someone had hung my saddle and my tack over her stall door. I fingered the long new brown girth.

'I know I checked it,' I said to nobody in particular.

'We believe you,' said Greg, 'the question is who loosened it?'

'What are you on about?' asked Lorcan.

'Who had both the motive and the opportunity?' said Greg.

'Camille,' Kylie suggested.

'She was stuck to my side like superglue since we got here,' said Lorcan.

'Are you sure?' said Greg.

'I think so,' said Lorcan, 'she might have gone to the bathroom or something for a couple of minutes.'

'Camille's no fan of mine but I don't think she'd try and get me killed and anyway, she's terrified of horses. I can't imagine her going anywhere near Luna,' I interjected.

'Anyone else wander off during the time Evie tacked up and went out for inspection?' asked Greg.

'That Coltan dude, the reception in the barn was terrible and he went out to text someone,' said Lorcan.

'Coltan never even remembers Evie's name,' said Greg, 'why would he want to hurt her?'

Nobody said anything for a few moments and I patted Luna's neck.

'Finn,' said Lorcan. 'He disappeared when Evie was in the stables.'

'It wasn't Finn,' Greg and I said quickly in unison.

'And he rescued me,' I pointed out.

'He didn't exactly rescue you,' said Lorcan. 'He could have put you in a wheelchair for life impulsively moving you like that. What if your neck had been broken? And it was none of his business, why doesn't he stick to looking after his own girlfriend?

We all looked at Lorcan in surprise; he's such a cool laid-back guy, it's not like him to bother to get angry and it's not like I'm his girlfriend.

'You don't know the first thing about my brother,' said Greg.

Lorcan shrugged.

'Come on, let's go back in and watch Tamara,' I said hastily, 'Scott will be here soon.'

'The attempted murder mystery will remain unsolved for now,' said Greg, typing some notes in the mini-iPad he had taken to carrying around.

# Chapter 10

We had our fourth snowstorm of the year a few days ago. The doormen are fed up with shoveling the snow from the sidewalk in front of our building. The snow is no longer pure or white or soft. It is a filthy forlorn grey, strewn with garbage, packed as hard as cement in banks along the edges of the sidewalks in Manhattan. On the corners of every block, the foot traffic has created deep holes in the snow filled with murky icy water. It's impossible to go anywhere in the city without trudging through them (or falling into them). In Ireland, a big snowstorm is such a rarity that it would bring the country to a standstill for a week. Schools and offices would close. Snow meant freedom. Here, it means more work for nearly everyone and lots of complaining on the subway about the Mayor of New York for not having the snow cleared up fast enough. Nothing is ever done fast enough for New Yorkers.

I have never felt cold like this. The cold burns on the inside and out and turns my lips blue. In the mornings on the way to school, I stop at a deli to buy a blue and white paper cup filled with grainy black coffee that tastes disgusting like lukewarm Bovril. But I don't buy it to drink, I buy it to hold when my fingers start to hurt, to bring some sensation back into my hands already enclosed in two pairs of gloves.

Holly insisted on giving me a pair of her earmuffs. They are unusually large, hairy and canary yellow. I didn't want to hurt her feelings by refusing them. My compassion towards her feelings does not extend to wearing those hideous earmuffs all the way to school. I always take them off and stow them in my schoolbag at least three blocks away. This morning, that safety precaution was sadly inadequate. Camille somehow managed to snap an extremely unflattering photograph of me in all the glory of my oversized yellow earmuffs, and had it up on Facebook before I even arrived at school. It was maddening.

Greg is also maddening. He thinks that Kylie likes Akono as in *like like*. That's ridiculous. Kylie is ALWAYS going on about the sacrifices she has to make in order to succeed in being famous one day. One of the biggest sacrifices is in the realm of personal romantic relationships. Kylie does not have time for boys. And anyway, even if she decided to break her own rules, she would never go for someone nice and normal like Akono.

When I arrived home from school today, Scott said we needed to have a talk. He said it in such a serious voice that I quickly scanned through my brain for crimes but I couldn't think of anything that bad, not recently anyway.

'You're not in any trouble,' said Scott, 'we just need to talk … about your dad.'

'You mean Michael,' I said (calling him my dad is just too

freaky).

'Yes, Michael,' said Scott, 'he's filed a lawsuit trying to claim custody of you.'

I blinked, confused. 'I know and your lawyer made it go away.'

'That was the idea,' said Scott, 'my lawyer made the application to get Michael's claims dismissed and we won. But Michael appealed and a bunch of four grumpy old men and one uptight old woman, the appeal judges, decided Michael can go ahead with his case, in the interests of justice or something like that. Some justice, huh!'

'What are you saying? Michael *won*? I have to leave New York and go live with a total stranger who could be a complete psycho.'

'No. No way. Not gonna happen!' said Scott. 'It just means we have to go through some more rounds in the court process.'

'How can you be so sure Michael won't win? I mean, last time, you made out it was all easy-peasy lemon squeezy. You said it was just like a *parking ticket* case. That's what you said.'

'I know I did,' Scott said quietly, 'that's what I thought. But trust me, there's no way any sane judge in the US of A is going to give custody to Michael.'

'But what if we don't get a sane judge? What if we get the craziest judge in America or some judge that takes bribes, like that judge out in Brooklyn that Joanna was talking about last year, remember, it was on Fox news. What if–'

'Whoa, Evie, breathe! It's going to work out. We have to take it one step at a time or *we're* the ones that will go nuts!'

'I can't believe this is happening,' I said, 'it's like a nightmare. How could those appeal judges let Michael do this? They've never even met us. Do they know I am THIRTEEN?'

Scott ran his hands through his hair.

'Yes, I guess so. I don't know. We will deal with all this. It's just going to take longer than we figured to get rid of this guy.'

'A trial,' I wailed, 'more lawyer stuff. Way more money. You can't afford this Scott. Maybe the best thing to do is for me to go back to Ireland for a while. I could stay with Janet's parents in Dingle in the middle of nowhere, just until Michael gives up and goes back to wherever he's been hiding for the last thirteen years.

'Hey, I don't want to hear talk like that. You. Me. Ben. We're a family. Remember! We'll get through this and the extra money from the Zoo will help pay the legal bills. Let's take things one at a time. First, you have to get a blood test done to see if this guy really is your Dad.'

Scott hugged me and I blinked back some tears. They were not tears of sadness. They were tears of pure rage with Michael and with the judges and with the whole stupid system. Could some New York judge ship me off to Australia like some poor, ancient convict who stole a loaf of bread because his family was starving? That was crazy.

Later that evening, when I finally got my head together a bit, I went out to meet Kylie and Greg at one of the huge multiplex cinemas at Times Square. I wasn't in the mood for watching a movie, but I didn't want to stay alone in my room either. I was late. Greg and Kylie were waiting for me in the lobby, having already loaded up on popcorn and nachos and super-size sodas. Akono was with them, which was a bit weird because he's older, Finn's friend, not ours. Kylie told me she guessed he didn't have anything better to do.

The movie was boring and excruciatingly long. It had been Greg's idea to see a zombie film anyway. I wanted to tell Kylie about what had happened, about Michael, but she was whispering to Akono the whole time. I kept trying to whisper my news to Greg but each time I said, 'Greg,' and he said 'what?' I said 'nothing.' After three times, he took off his 3-D glasses and said that I was making him miss all the best blood and gore parts of the movie so there was no point in bothering to watch it. I said 'sorry,' and he put the glasses back on and I gave him my popcorn because I wasn't hungry.

I couldn't concentrate on what was happening on the screen. My head was spinning crazily with my own home-made movies, in the horror genre. In my imagination, Michael won the custody trial and shipped me off to work as a slave in the deep, dark, suffocating, filthy darkness of a tin mine in the Australian outback where I would probably die in a year or so as a result of being smothered by a cave-in. I knew I was thinking crazy thoughts. Do they even mine tin in Australia? But I couldn't get my head to switch off. I couldn't even switch the channel or turn the volume down. My mind was stuck, thinking whatever stupid scary thoughts it wanted to think. It didn't care about what I wanted to think about. As the closing credits rolled, Greg glanced at me,

'Are you ok?' he asked.

I nodded.

'You're dripping with sweat and you look pale,' he said.

'I'm fine, I'm just tired,' I said and I thought, maybe Michael is one of those weird twisted maniacs that will make me sleep in a coffin and live on a diet of meagre scraps, like a poor neglected dog that is blind in one eye.

Holly texted me to say Scott had an emergency call from the zoo and he'd asked her to come meet me. I'm not allowed to take the subway at night by myself and Kylie and Greg both live on the East Side. Akono offered to take Kylie home, which is totally out of his way because he lives down in Battery Park City. Greg whispered to me,

'I told you there's something going on between those two.'

He didn't say it in a smug, I-told-you-so voice, more like a resigned, and now, we can say goodbye to Kylie forever tone. Greg reads too much into things.

Holly talked the whole way on the subway home, but I wasn't really listening. There were advertisements plastered along the top of the subway carriage – for a personal injury law firm in New Jersey, a cosmetic dental surgeon in the Bronx and for a *Learn English Fast* course in Bayside in Queens. The New Jersey law firm advert consisted of a photograph of a man with dyed black hair in a cheap grey suit with a phony smile, holding up a cheque as big as a chair with a lot of zeroes on it. 'This could be you,' the ad promised.

That lawyer could be him, I thought, my dad. He could be anyone. He could be sitting here in the same subway carriage as me and I wouldn't know. He could be watching me right now and I wouldn't know. I looked around the half-full subway feeling creeped out, but nobody was remotely interested in me; their eyes were on the floor or on their phones or closed with exhaustion. Nobody looks more tired than a New York subway-rider.

Holly said something about my dad. That caught my attention and I turned to look at her.

'What was that?' I said.

'Don't be hard on Scottie for not telling you about your dad's appeal, he's just trying to do what's best for you,' Holly said, 'although you know, it's real nice, sugar, that you have a dad who is interested in having you.'

It made me feel SO mad that Holly, a practical stranger, the part-time receptionist, had obviously known all about the appeal when I hadn't known a thing.

'Yeah, whatever,' I said rudely, 'interested after thirteen years.'

'Better late than never, sugar,' said Holly and I rolled my eyes.

'Yeah, that and a thousand other oh-so-comforting clichés, thank you so much,' I said, 'that was super helpful and incredibly useful.'

Holly stopped talking, which isn't like her at all. She took a hand mirror out of her purse, the size of a small suitcase and began fixing her hair.

'And don't call him my DAD,' I practically shouted at her. She twirled a strand of her yellow hair around one of her fingers and didn't answer.

I felt a sharp pain in my stomach. I might have a stone in my gallbladder, I thought hopefully, remembering the terrible pain David, my mum's friend, had in his stomach the Easter before last. But really, I knew perfectly well, my gallbladder was pebble-free. The pain was just my totally deserved guilt for being such a horrible mean brat and to a genuinely sweet person like Holly who was only trying to help me. How low could I go?

'I'm so sorry Holly for being such a big pain in the butt,' I said hoarsely, 'I'm just kind of mad with everyone today. I hate that guy, Michael, for messing around in our lives.'

Holly smiled at me, a genuine wide smile, instantly forgiving me and I felt even more remorseful. I pushed my hair back from my eyes.

'You grew up without your dad?' I asked.

Holly laughed and shook her head. 'Hell, no, his trailer was in the same park as ours; I saw him all the time but that loser never had any interest in me. He wasn't interested in anyone, not even himself, the only thing he cared about was beer.'

'Sounds awful,' I said.

'Nah, it wasn't too bad, he didn't cause trouble, he was a weak man, not a bad one.'

I didn't know what to say about that. I started thinking about Michael again. Holly glanced at me and said,

'Boy, am I jealous of Joanna lazing around in Mexico or

somewhere having fun while we're freezing our little butts off here in subzero temperatures.'

'Joanna wouldn't even know how to *begin* to laze around,' I said. 'Scott and I are so good at it. Joanna's with Jeffrey; they've gone on a field trip to Texas. It's a working volunteer holiday. They're helping to record the current numbers of the Braken Bat Cave Meshweaver.'

'Joanna has gone to some stinky cave with bats to weave nets?' asked Holly in a horrified voice, glancing quickly around the subway carriage as if to expecting to see vampire bats drop down from the ceiling.

'No, a Braken Bat Cave Meshweaver is a spider. It's a very difficult name and I don't think it was a bright idea to have the words 'Bat Cave,' in a spider name; you are bound to think of bats! '

'Why would anyone want to spend their vacation time counting spiders,' asked Holly with a shudder.

'They're an endangered species,' I explained.

Joanna had shown me a photograph of the spider last week – a jelly-pink, flesh-coloured, almost transparent blobby thing that looks like a naked spider foetus. I nearly screamed when I saw it. 'That thing is disgusting,' I had said truthfully. Joanna said that it is easy to be a wildlife enthusiast when it comes to the 'cute' animals. 'Yes, it is,' I'd agreed.

Walking home from our subway stop on 72$^{nd}$ Street, Holly kept insisting that Joanna and Jeffrey were really on sun loungers knocking back margaritas in Cancun. Holly doesn't know Joanna very well because she hates sunbathing.

And, Holly certainly doesn't know Joanna's boyfriend, Jeffrey. He hasn't taken a real vacation since he was twelve or at least, that's what he told Scott. He bragged about it like that was a good thing.

By the time Holly and I reached home I felt in a much better mood and totally distracted by the whole spider/Joanna/Jeffrey tangents. It was only much later after Holly had gone home and I was in bed that I wondered if Holly had deliberately distracted me from thinking about Michael and the custody case. I think – probably yes and it had worked, I felt in control of my mind again, which was a huge relief. Holly is much smarter than she sometimes gets credit for.

# Chapter 11

$\mathcal{S}$unday is my least favourite day of the week. It's a long, boring chunk of time you have to pass through until school on Monday morning. It's like treading water during swimming class. Almost every single second of Sunday, I'm horribly aware that I should be doing my weekend homework, but Sundays are depressing enough without throwing homework into the mix. I think we should all get credit for just surviving them.

It's different for Scott because he watches football every Sunday night so he actually looks forward to them. I don't feel up to the challenge of learning the rules of American football this year; I still have not fully mastered baseball.

Today, however, was no ordinary, simply surviving Sunday. It began with an emergency. Greg had taken Dr Pepper for some fresh air in Central Park and somehow, somewhere, Dr Pepper had vanished. Yep. One average-sized, black rabbit alone in the wilds of Central Park. That might not sound terribly alarming but coyotes have been spotted in the Park this year.

Kylie was at her ice-skating class so as soon as I got off the phone with a panicked Greg, I called Lorcan to come help.

We met at the Delacorte Theatre near my end of the Park, which was the meeting point for all the volunteer rescuers. Finn took charge of the rescue efforts. He brought a bunch of maps of the Park, which had been divided into quadrants and he assigned all of the volunteers a different quadrant to search. Tamara couldn't come because she had to study for some big test, but her twin brother, Coltan, whom I still can't stand, was there, which didn't make any sense as he's the last person in the world to care about a missing rabbit. He hung around close to Finn, making a lot of surprisingly helpful and clever suggestions about organising the search. I wasn't buying it. Coltan never reaches out to help anyone unless there's something in it for him. He must want something from Finn but God knows what that is. A bunch of kids from school turned up to help and Luke and Luca, a pair of identical twins from Greg's *Young Film-Makers of Tomorrow* class. Angela, Greg's mom, came along with her boyfriend, Leonard. She brought flasks of hot chocolate for us, the really good, double-chocolatey kind from Dean & DeLuca.

The last time I saw Finn, I was in his arms, being carried out of the arena after I flew over Luna's head. The whole carrying business only lasted a few minutes but I had replayed it so many times in my mind that I felt a rush of embarrassment when I saw Finn. I had to keep clearing my throat because it felt like there was a big clump of oatmeal stuck in it. Finn spoke to me very casually as if the incident never happened. Clearly, he has not been replaying anything in his mind.

He assigned Lorcan and me the area around the reservoir in the north of the Park to search.

'That's not my favourite section of the Park,' Lorcan said.

'Me neither,' I said.

'If Dr Pepper fell into the reservoir, I'm sure it's not his favourite section either,' Finn replied.

'What?' gulped Greg. 'Fell into the reservoir. Dr Pepper can't swim! Remember I put him in the bath tub that time—'

'Keep it together Greg,' said Finn, 'I was kidding. Dr Pepper isn't in a watery grave. He's far too smart. We'll find him.'

'Yes of course we will, Greg,' I said, heading off to start the search.

Finn called after me. 'Why don't you like the reservoir, Evie?'

I stopped and looked back and shrugged.

'It always seems a little lost and lonely, an outsider who doesn't really belong in Central Park and secretly wishes it had been built in some provincial town in Canada.'

I thought Finn would laugh, but he didn't. He just nodded almost imperceptibly and turned back to the maps.

Lorcan and I set off in opposite directions around the reservoir, expecting to meet somewhere in the middle. Central Park is a very big area in which to find one black rabbit enjoying a bid for freedom. I hustled around the reservoir, poking in the foliage with a stick and calling out Dr Pepper's name, which was kind of dumb because he's never come in response to his name before. Even though it was super cold and big slushy snowflakes were falling lightly, there were loads of joggers and skaters around. New Yorkers aren't nosey at all. Nobody stopped me and asked, 'Hey, what are you looking for, kid?'

About one-third of the way around the reservoir, I saw Finn walking towards me, a bundle of black fur in his arms.

'Dr Pepper, Yay! You found him!' I said.

'Not me. Some kids found him,' said Finn, 'he'd been trapped under one of the wooden rowing boats, stored upside down for winter and managed to tunnel his way out. The Great Rabbit Escape. I've texted Greg,' added Finn. 'He'll meet us by the Wollman rink. Come on.'

'Ok, let me just text Lorcan to let him know Dr Pepper is alive and hungry and to head for the Wollman rink.'

After sending the text, I fell into step beside Finn. I had to take two steps for every one of his to keep up with him so I felt a little like a trotting pony. Finn seemed to notice because he slowed down a little. Isn't it funny how even walking beside someone, not saying anything at all, can be so … intense? I noticed he had had a haircut since I last saw him. His coat sleeves rode up a little and I could see the thin white scars on his left arm. Finn had told me he got those scars from playing ice hockey but Greg told me once that their biological Mom's drug-dealer-boyfriend used to beat Finn. I don't blame Finn for lying about what must have been a super crappy childhood before he and Greg were adopted by the Winters.

'So how are things going, Evie?' Finn asked.

'Great,' I said.

'I heard about the whole my-dad-is-a-terrorist-from-Iceland thing at school,' said Finn with his half-smile.

'Oh, yeah. That was centuries ago. Everyone seems to have forgotten about that now. Stale news. Now, they're talking about some kid who was found living in the girls' bathroom on the third floor. But I bet that kid doesn't exist. It's probably a particularly large and active cockroach.'

'Imagine your Dad really was a terrorist,' said Finn, 'You don't know, he could be anywhere doing anything.'

'Not really,' I said, 'he's actually here in Manhattan fighting Scott in court to get custody of me.'

'What?' asked Finn, 'are you for real?'

'No, I mean, yes, my so-called Dad's camped out in some hotel uptown. He just turned up at the clinic one day and seemed to think we'd have peanut butter and jelly sandwiches together and … and I don't know, go bowling or something. Scott told him to take a hike. I haven't told Greg and Kylie yet, but I will.'

'Let's sit here for a minute,' said Finn pointing at a bench half-hidden under some snow-laden pine trees. It would have been prettier if it wasn't so cold. Way too cold to sit down, I thought but I swept some snow off the bench and sat down. Finn put Dr Pepper on the ground and stood in front of me, very close, keeping Dr Pepper gripped between his ankles. Without warning, he leaned forward and brushed my hair with his hand. I jumped as if he had tasered me.

'You had snow in your hair,' he explained.

'Oh,' I said very intelligently.

'So, wow, your deadbeat dad's rolled into town. What's he like?' he asked.

'I don't know,' I said, 'I don't want to meet him. I haven't even seen him and with even a teeny bit of luck and Scott's lawyer, I never will.'

'You're crazy,' Finn said bluntly.

I stiffened, feeling horribly hurt and offended.

'Bet you wouldn't want to see your mum who abandoned you,' I said.

'You'd lose that bet,' said Finn. 'Mom had lots of bad luck. It was her stupid dealer, every time she tried to get herself clean and move us away, he would find her, and come around. He was always there. He wouldn't let her go. I hope she beat it, that she's clean now wherever she is.'

'Clean?' I said.

'Free from drugs,' he explained.

There was a silence. I was still smarting at being called crazy. I opened my big fat stupid mouth.

'Druggies don't change,' I snapped.

Finn's dark eyes flashed and I will never ever forget the look he gave me. He looked at me as if he didn't know me. After a couple of seconds he said,

'You're just a kid brought up in some cute, artsy Bohemian lifestyle in Ireland. You have no idea what you're talking about.'

'Hey, there you guys are! I've been waiting for you forever

at the rink!' yelled Greg.

He ran over and scooped up Dr Pepper and began to examine him. Dr Pepper didn't seem any the worse for his tunneling misadventures except for being very dirty. Coltan sauntered up wearing the artificial grin he keeps permanently plastered on his smooth face. He looked slyly at me and at Finn and then back at me again and he smirked a little. Without so much as a 'see ya', Finn walked off with him, leaving me sitting there on a very cold bench, staring at the shoelaces in my boots as if they were the most interesting things I had ever seen.

For the rest of the day, I couldn't stop replaying the conversation with Finn over and over in my head giving us both different dialogue each time. I don't know why I said what I did. The worst part is I don't even believe it. I'm sure people can change. I mean, it's really, really hard, but it's possible. All the thinking was totally exhausting. When your thoughts whirl around in circles, they tend to suck all your energy into the pool in the middle, leaving you feeling drained and empty. I spent hours trying to write a text to Finn to try and apologise. Everything I wrote seemed so wrong and stiff or else it was inappropriately silly and jokey. In the end, just before eight o'clock, I texted: 'Hi, I'm sorry for saying that stupid thing today. Evie'

Then I stared at my phone waiting for a reply. It was AGONY. I was incapable of doing anything but stare at my phone, waiting and waiting and then waiting some more. A solid two hours later, a few minutes after 10, Finn sent a text back: 'k'

That was it, just 'k.' He must hate me. No, worse than that. He doesn't care what I think.

# Chapter 12

When the blood test result came back stating that Michael Carey was my biological father with a 99.97 per cent probability, I wasn't surprised, I wasn't really anything, kind of numb, I suppose. I *was* shocked when Scott told me that the *Court* had appointed a lawyer for me. It made me imagine that the words 'EVIE BROOKS SHALL HAVE A LAWYER,' appeared overnight in white chalk on the ceiling of some court building.

Scott got an email from my lawyer scheduling our first meeting for 10 on a Wednesday in a conference room, 4G, in the Family Law Court on Lafayette Street. At least, I got to miss double math, which I have every Wednesday morning under Mr Papadopoulos's excessively-hairy nostrils.

Scott and I took the A subway downtown and walked the rest of the way to the courthouse. We got there in plenty of time, around 9:30. The line of people (mainly women and kids) stretched out the double glass doors and around the block, nearly to the Starbucks on the corner. We shuffled forward excruciatingly slowly towards the security checks. Nobody in the line made a sound, not even the toddler in a stroller patched together with duct tape.

By the time we made it to the front of the line and through security and retrieved our shoes and Scott had put his belt back on, it was a few minutes to ten. Scott took one look at the silent huddle of people waiting resignedly at the elevator bank and decided we'd be quicker taking the stairs. I think we both regretted those breakfast burritos.

My lawyer, Marcy, was waiting for us. There was a dwarfish quality about her. She was not much bigger than me, with rather messy mousy hair and big glasses with peach frames. She wore a navy and black checked trouser suit stained with what looked like mayonnaise on the right lapel.

Conference Room 4G was small room with just enough space for a small table and two plastic chairs. There was a sprinkling of used staples on the table and a couple of pieces of torn paper. The only picture on the walls was a black and white poster advertising HIV counseling services. The room smelt faintly of despair and spicy chicken empanadas.

'You must be Evangeline,' Marcy said, shaking my hand.

'Hi,' I said, 'call me Evie.'

Then she said to Scott, 'You can pick her up in half an hour.'

'I'll stay with her,' he said.

'No,' said Marcy, 'I need to speak to my client alone. You can wait out in the hallway.'

It took me a few seconds to realise I was the 'client,' she was talking about. I said, 'It's ok,' to Scott and he said he'd wait right outside.

Marcy and I sat down on the two chairs and she fumbled

in her briefcase and pulled out two thick velobound bundles of paper, which she placed on the desk. She scooted her chair around to bring it much closer to mine and I had to resist the impulse to push my chair back further. She smiled very widely at me. She had dark burgundy lipstick on one of her front teeth.

'Evie,' she said, 'I'm a lawyer that represents children. We used to be called law guardians but now we're just called lawyers for the child.'

'Em, ok, that's nice,' I said inanely.

She smiled again. The lipstick stain had spread to a second tooth. 'I love representing children, so that I can give them a voice,' she said.

I didn't say anything to that. I'm thirteen, not a child and I have a voice of my own and I can make it very loud when I feel like it.

Marcy showed me photographs on her phone of her three-year-old twin boys. I said, 'They look cute,' and passed her phone back. I guessed that she was trying to 'bond' with me but I didn't feel bonded with Marcy because she happened to have pushed out some kids of her own. Why should I? I wondered when we would get to the part about why I was there. Maybe Marcy sensed that because she put her phone away and said,

'Like I said, I'm your lawyer. I will be representing you in connection with the litigation. Your biological father wants to have custody of you and your uncle, Dr Brooks, wants to retain custody. Everything you say to me is confidential. Do you understand that?'

'Yes,' I said.

'You are the boss. I must follow your instructions. Whatever you tell me to do, I have to do it, unless I feel that you are not capable of making decisions in your own best interests, in which case, I can decide how best to act for you.'

I didn't like the sound of that at all.

'What do you mean?' I asked.

'Don't worry about it,' said Marcy, 'you seem pretty sharp and I'm sure it will never happen that I have to substitute my judgment for yours. That happens very rarely.'

Then she began to talk about the case. She talked solidly for about twenty minutes, all about what a custody case involves and what might or might not happen and about the other cases she has had and how well she did in them. Marcy said the judge in my case is the Honourable Susanna Flicker, and she's one of the screamer judges, but I wasn't to worry about that because she knows how to handle *Psycho Suzie*. I didn't find that very reassuring.

It was all quite confusing but I didn't get the opportunity to ask any more questions. There was a knock on the door and a fat man with a face like a bull mastiff, came in and said, 'Marcy, I really need to talk to you now about the settlement in the Polowski case,' and she said, 'Fine, I'll be right with you,' and she went out the door with him, leaving me alone in the room. There was nothing to do and nothing to look at. Ten minutes later, Marcy came back and she talked some more, this time about the father in the Polowski case, who she said was a cheap alcoholic.

I wasn't interested in Mr Polowski's issues. Finally, I interrupted her and said,

'Just to be clear, I don't want anything to do with Michael at all. I want to stay with Scott.'

Marcy reached out and rubbed my hand as if I were a five-year-old and asked me if I had a therapist to help me work through my feelings. I told her that I know what my feelings are. I don't want to see Michael. I don't want anything to do with him. Then she looked at her Blackberry and said she had leave to pick up her kids but that she would see me again soon. I wished she had written down what I had said but I guess it's not difficult to remember. As we went through the door, she gave me a card with her phone number and email address on it and said, 'remember, you're on Team Marcy now.'

'Thanks,' I said, which was a bit cowardly of me because what I felt like saying was, 'I don't want to be on Team Marcy or any other team. I just want all this stupid legal stuff to be over.'

Scott was waiting outside, leaning up against a wall with his hands in his pockets. I could tell from the way his hair was standing up in spikes that he'd been anxiously running his hands through it. He looked as eager to get out there as I did. I think it was the atmosphere. It's one of those places where you feel — nothing good happens here — nothing much of anything happens here, only waiting and waiting. But the security guards all seemed very friendly and nice;

almost apologetic that you had to be there as if it was their fault.

It was a 'B' week so Greg was living with his mom in the East Village. I went over there to hang out that evening with him and Kylie. I told them about my Dad turning up and about my meeting with Marcy. Greg was astounded and a little hurt that I hadn't said anything before. But Kylie was surprisingly ok about it. She said she understood that sometimes you have to keep stuff to yourself for a little while until you figure it out. They didn't think Marcy sounded too impressive. They asked a lot of questions about Michael. I explained that Scott and I only knew what Rob, Scott's lawyer had told us – Michael lives in Melbourne in Australia and is married to a woman named Emily.

'Oh and he's some kind of music producer,' I added.

'OMG,' said Kylie, 'your long-lost dad is a famous, billionaire music producer!'

'No,' I said a little testily, 'he was never lost and he's not a billionaire although he does make a LOT more money than Scott and before you ask, I don't know what acts he produces and I don't care.'

'Sorry,' said Kylie.

'That's ok,' I said and then I very pointedly changed the subject by asking Greg about his infected mosquito bite. It's pretty amazing to get a mosquito bite in winter.

# Chapter 13

**E**arly this morning before school, because Holly called in sick, I was in the unenviable position of having to inform Scott that Mrs Rubenstein was in the waiting room. He grimaced before asking cheerlessly,

'Which cat is it this time that I am supposed to have poisoned?'

'I don't know,' I said, 'she didn't bring any of her cats with her; she says she wants a *hands-off* consultation.'

'What does that even mean?' sighed Scott. 'Ok, send her in and if she doesn't reemerge in ten minutes, I want you to run in here and scream "fire" as loudly as you can. You think you can do that?'

'Sure, I got it, Fire, Scream, Everyone Out.'

He nodded, 'and I'm not kidding!'

'I know,' I said. It might seem a little drastic but only if you have never met Mrs Rubenstein.

Back out in the waiting room, Mrs Rubenstein had pointedly moved her chair as far away as possible from the young couple with the small, shaggy, white dog wearing a spiked collar. The couple sat together quietly holding hands. They had matching tattoos of fire-breathing purple and orange dragons on their pale inner arms. Both of them had a lot of piercings on their eyebrows, noses and lips and when the girl yawned, a shiny silvery stud flashed on her tongue.

'You can go through to Dr Brooks now Mrs Rubenstein,' I said and with a parting dismissive sniff at the young couple, she donned a clear plastic glove on her right hand to touch the door handle.

'Hi,' said the girl to me. Her hair was long on the right side and shaved on the other. 'I'm Nikki and this is Max and Eddie.'

'Hi,' I said, 'what's the problem with Max?'

The young man grinned. 'I'm Max and there's plenty wrong with me. But we're here about Eddie; he's got a cough,' he said patting the dog.

'What kind of dog is Eddie?' I asked curiously.

'He's a Westiepoo.'

'A what?'

'Westiepoo,' repeated Nikki, 'a West Highland White Terrier/Poodle mix. I'm pretty much obsessed with poos.'

'We have plenty of that round here,' I said, 'so you've come to the right place.'

'You might have worded that better, Nikki,' said Max and she laughed.

'I'm obsessed with poodle hybrids,' Nikki explained. 'When Max and I were looking for a dog, we checked out Pekeapoos, Pomapoos, Cockapoos, Bossi-Poos, Airedoodles, Boonoodles, a Foxhoodle and two Double Doodles.'

'Yeah,' said Max, 'and don't forget the Pinny-Poo, the

Poogle, the Pomapoo and the Woodle.'

'A Woodle? I said.

'Yep,' said Nikki, 'it's a cross between a Soft Coated Wheaten Terrier and a Poodle, and we also got the train to Rhode Island to visit a Bolonoodle and a Cadoodle'.

'You guys are making this up!' I said.

They both grinned.

'Nope,' said Max, 'there's a whole words of poos and doodles out there. We're going to get a Schnoodle next to keep Eddie company.'

The conversation was so interesting that I temporarily forgot about Scott being trapped with Mrs Rubenstein preaching to him about her makey-uppy theories on cat illnesses.

'Yikes' I said, when I noticed the time. I was just about to scream 'fire,' and run into the examining room when Scott appeared in the doorway practically pushing Mrs Rubenstein in front of him, a dazed expression on his face.

Mrs Rubenstein had a bunch of fliers in her hands.

'I will leave my brochures for my upcoming seminar at your reception,' she said, handing them to me.

'How very kind,' said Scott.

I glanced at the brochures advertising Mrs Rubenstein's workshop for kitty lovers whose partners are not of the same persuasion. They seemed to advocate divorce as the most practical solution.

'Leave them with us, Mrs Rubenstein, Good-bye,' Scott added firmly,

'Who do we have next, Evie?

'Eddie the Westiepoo,' I said.

It turned out that Eddie just had kennel cough, which is highly contagious. Scott reckoned Eddie had picked it up from another dog when he was boarded in a kennel last week while Max and Nikki were in Vegas attending a convention for tattoo artists. Scott said the cough should disappear in about three weeks and he reminded Nikki and Max about keeping Eddie's vaccinations up to date.

When she was paying the fee, Nikki insisted on giving Scott a voucher for a free tattoo at their parlour in the East Village.

Ben trotted into the waiting room.

'Your dog is super cute,' said Nikki, 'we could do a life-size tattoo of him on your chest. We'd have to shave your chest first.'

'Thanks,' said Scott, 'but I'm not sure that will do wonders for my romantic life and I see enough of Ben as it is without having him in the shower with me.'

Nikki smiled. 'We have plenty of other animal tattoos. A lot of our customers ask for tattoos of their pets. Unicorn tattoos are probably the most popular.'

'We don't see a lot of unicorns in this practice,' said Scott, 'I guess we're too far uptown.'

Max laughed and picked Eddie up, 'Come on, Nikki, bye, Dr Brooks, if you change your mind about getting a tattoo, come see us. I've also been getting into taxidermy lately. Did a great job for a customer whose cat died. His stuffed cat now resides on top of his TV.'

My mouth dropped open. I didn't like the thought of dead stuffed animals on top of the TV or anywhere else.

After they had gone, I asked Scott,

'Could we use the voucher to get me a tiny tattoo of a barn owl on my ankle?'

'No,' said Scott, and he didn't say it in a *no but maybe if you push, I will change my mind, kind of way*, it was a no of the unequivocal kind, a non-negotiable one. I shrugged. Tattoos aren't that cool. Most of the adults I know have at least one. I told Scott about Megan, a girl in my geography class, who has her name tattooed on her wrist although they spelt it wrong so it says 'Megen.' Scott said that if you need to look at your wrist to be reminded of your name, you have real problems to worry about.

# Chapter 14

Marcy called to suggest that I get a haircut before we had to go to court.

Bewildered, I asked her, 'What difference does it make to the judge what my hair looks like?'

'Appearances matter,' she said airily, 'Ask the hairdressers to do something. Think less wild child, more Laura Ingalls.'

'Who?' I asked.

'Never mind,' she said.

But I think Marcy had made a fair point on the wild-child hair. Kylie, more considerately, refers to it as my *uniquely-relaxed style*.

Kylie's Mom, Rachel, took us to a hair salon on West 83rd Street. It was my first haircut in Manhattan, not counting the time last year Scott cruelly chopped a great big lump out of my hair when I had a massive knot. Kylie had very specific ideas about what kind of style she wanted. Her hairdresser, Shoshanna, looked a little overwhelmed when Kylie handed her a detailed sketch plus three different pictures cut out from magazines. But she was a professional. She circled Kylie, lifting up locks of her hair and said, thoughtfully, 'Yes, I can work within the general parameters of the sketch and these pictures but perhaps keeping the middle parting.'

'No, no,' said Kylie, looking very distressed. 'I'm not doing a good job of explaining – the sketch and the pictures are examples of what I DON'T want my hair to turn out like.'

'Feel free to adopt her' said Rachel to Shoshanna before she left to return to her gallery.

The atmosphere in the salon reminded me of the theatre. There were lots of glamorous people wearing cool clothes, rushing around, looking important and gossiping. I felt the thrill of the impending rise of the curtain, like a play was about to be performed. The clean, fresh smell of expensive shampoo and anticipation wafted through the salon. It smelled much better than the theatre, which usually reeks of sweaty old tights and nervousness.

They sat Kylie and me in high adjustable red leather chairs with a chair between us. A hairdresser was hard at work on highlights for the customer who sat between us. I couldn't stop staring because the customer was particularly unusual; it was just the head of a mannequin with a long wig of honey blond hair. I thought that the hairdresser must be training. Kylie said it might be a wig for a cancer victim and I felt bad. My hairdresser, a guy from Estonia called André, who wore black and red boots with very high heels, explained that a lot of the salon's customers were Hasidic Jews.

'Nobody is allowed to see their real hair except their husbands,' he said.

'Like Muslim women who wear veils,' said Kylie.

'I suppose so,' said André, looking surprised.

'Why do they wear wigs?' I asked.

André shrugged. 'I think it has something to do with modesty – avoiding vanity.'

'But that wig is gorgeous,' I said.

'Celebrity level,' Andre agreed in a worshipful voice. 'The customers are very fussy and proud of their wigs. They spend thousands of dollars on them. You wouldn't believe how competitive they can be about them.'

I found the wig a little creepy.

After we had our hair cut, we had to wait a few minutes for blow-drys. (They call them blowouts, which I found appropriate, considering how expensive everything was). It was cheap of me but I felt bad about having three people to tip instead of one – the woman who washed my hair, André who cut it, and, now someone new would come along to dry it. I whispered to Kylie about my dilemma and she pointed out, 'and, there's the woman who took our coats, she'll be expecting a tip as well.'

'Scott would be able to buy a new Jeep for the cost of my haircut,' I moaned dramatically to Kylie but she was absorbed with her phone.

'Look, Akono just texted me a picture of a baby riding a scooter, it's the cutest thing.'

She leaned over to pass her phone to me. As I fumbled to reach it, the folds of my overlong black gown knocked against the freshly-wigged mannequin head sending it crashing to the floor. The wig fell off and the head rolled like a ball in a bowling alley halfway across the salon until it lodged between the ankles of an elderly woman having her hair washed. She didn't seem to notice.

Kylie and I stared in horror and we both jumped to pick up the wig. In the process, one of us stepped on it. I strongly suspect that was me because a wad of grey gooey chewing gum stuck to the bottom of my shoe somehow got entangled in the wig. The more Kylie and I tried to extract the gum, the more entangled it became. It was a total *nightmare*.

'Perhaps the woman who owns the wig could wear a lot of hats; they are really *in* this season,' said Kylie.

I glared at her.

André sauntering by our chairs, spotted the wig and screamed, a horrible high-pitched scream of pure panic, like a starlet in the opening scene of a horror film. Still screaming, he ran off and returned a few minutes later with the manager, Dmitri, a squat, muscular man with a gleaming, oiled bald head and bulging black eyes. I don't know if his eyes normally bulged or if that was just a reaction to the situation.

I placed the wig on a chair, and, rather hopelessly, patted some of the gooey strands.

'I'm very, very sorry,' I said, 'it was an accident.'

'An accident,' repeated Dmitri, 'an accident! That's a ten thousand dollar wig!'

Gulp. 'Ten THOUSAND dollars! For a wig? Just a wig, not a pair of kidneys thrown in?' I asked, and I wasn't being sarcastic. Not completely.

In a hoarse, rasping voice, Dmitri moaned,

'How am I going to explain this to Serena?'

Kylie patted Dmitri comfortingly on his arm.

'What about insurance?' she said, 'the wig is probably covered by her home insurance. My Mom's necklace got robbed three years ago and Mom said that we could have gotten money for it on our home insurance – if we had had home insurance, which we didn't at the time, but we do now. Nothing has been stolen since we got the insurance, which is pretty maddening.'

Dmitri shot her a murderous look. But it takes a lot to silence Kylie.

'Or you could just cut the gum out. It's mainly on the bottom and you could create a new style for Serena, maybe an Anna Wintour bob, they are always chic and timeless.'

André and Dmitri exchanged glances.

'I could try that,' said Andre.

'I'll help you,' I offered.

'NO,' shouted Dmitri, 'you kids have done enough. If this gets out, the reputation of my salon will be ruined forever. Just, get out of here, immediately, before you set the place on fire!'

'But we have to pay the tips,' I protested.

Another bloodcurdling scream ripped through the air. The elderly woman at the washbasin had become conscious that what she thought was a footrest was, in fact, a human head. I suppose she didn't realise it was a mannequin. They are incredibly lifelike.

We took that scream as our cue to make a fast exit.

Once outside, Kylie pointed out that now, I didn't have to worry about tipping. She deserves some kind of medal for always looking on the bright side. I could see a bright side too. I looked older with my new haircut. I could probably pass for fifteen in daylight now.

# Chapter 15

Getting out of having to go to school on a weekday is obviously a cause for celebration. On the downside, I'd prefer to be in school than heading to my first day in court. I was scared. So was Scott. I could tell from the way he made scrambled eggs for breakfast, but forgot to scramble them so they turned out more like eggy pancakes. That reminded me so much of Mum it hurt. That's exactly the kind of thing she did when she was nervous or scared. Scott, however, pretended that he wasn't nervous or scared at all; he kept singing snatches of rock songs and acting like it's normal for us to go to court. I pretended it was normal too.

Scott's lawyer told him to wear a dark conservative suit with a tie. So he wore the black Hugo Boss suit that he had worn to Mum's funeral. He smelled of tea-tree shower gel and aftershave.

Marcy called last night to tell me that I should look as old as I could because the older I look, the more the judge will be inclined to give 'weight' to my wishes. But she also told to not wear shoes with heels or a short skirt or make-up or anything revealing. I was glad she hadn't noticed I don't have much of anything to reveal yet.

I was happy with my new, more sophisticated haircut but the rest of my efforts were pretty much epic fail. I tried my best but when I looked in the mirror, I realised I had only succeeded in making myself look younger. The freckles on my nose were the main problem. Marcy had warned me not to chew gum or wear a baseball cap. I thought that was ridiculous.

I asked, 'What kind of person would do those things in court?'

Marcy said, 'Plenty! You'd be surprised!'

While Scott was yakking on the phone about a cat with cataracts, I discreetly slid my egg pancake into Ben's food bowl. Just as we are about to leave, Joanna came upstairs from the clinic to wish us luck. She hugged me and then turned to Scott. She stepped towards him and for a second or two, I thought she was about to hug him as well but she busied herself with adjusting one of his cuff links. They were in the shape of tiny silver motorbikes, a present from her to him the Christmas before last. Her hair looked even redder against the crisp whiteness of his shirt. There was an awkward hard-to-miss tension in the air that made me feel like slinking out of the room.

Scott broke it.

'So what cause is *speaking* to Jeffrey today?' he asked in what I think he meant to be a cheery casual tone but it sounded brittle and fake.

I rolled my eyes. Joanna stepped back, looking annoyed. She ignored his question.

'Good luck, guys!' she said briskly, 'I have to get back to the clinic.'

We watched her go back downstairs in silence.

'Don't say a word!' Scott groaned to me, 'Let's go.'

'Ok,' I said.

I wished Joanna was coming with us. So did Scott but he was too stubborn to say so.

With a final pat for Ben, we left. We didn't head for the Family Court on Lafayette Street because last month, the case was transferred to the Supreme Court of the State of New York. I don't know why. Everyone else just says the 'court', but I like saying the full title. I like the ringing sound of it; it sounds solid and like something the founding fathers would have approved of – not just any old court but the *Supreme* Court, and not just any ole Hicksville, nobody-can-remember-its-capital state, but *the* Empire State, THE STATE OF NEW YORK. Rob, Scott's lawyer, said that the case being transferred to the Supreme Court was a good thing because it's faster than the Family Court and the judges are smarter and they even sometimes know the law and apply it. Scott said he hasn't seen any evidence of this so far. But I thought any judge we got must be better than Psycho Suzie.

The courthouse sits at the top of the steps at 60 Centre Street, close to City Hall. It is huge and grey and commanding and resembles one of those ancient buildings you see in history books. I'd seen the stone steps plenty of times on T.V. It felt strange to be walking up them myself, like I had a part as an extra in a *Law and Order* episode.

There were two long lines at security, one for the lawyers and the judges and the clerks and the other for everyone else. Our line took much longer. When we finally cleared security, we found ourselves in a nearly empty, round, light-filled room with a high domed roof. It felt like being in a museum, but not MOMA, more like the Metropolitan. We wandered around the outer circumference of the circle looking for the right bank of elevators. A nice security guard showed us and pressed the button.

We met our lawyers, Marcy and Rob, outside the judge's courtroom on the fifth floor. They signed in with some security lady at a desk and then we walked through a pair of heavy wooden double doors. The courtroom looked pretty much like it does on TV. It was large and spacious with the US flag hanging limply on a brass flagpole on a raised platform beside the enormous desk where the judge sits. In front of the judge's desk, there was a smaller desk, where a young woman with blonde hair typed on a computer. She never looked up. Nearby, a young man with round glasses, sat in front of a weird looking tin box machine that had a thin ream of paper coming out of it.

'Who's that guy?' I asked Marcy.

'The stenographer,' she said.

'Huh?'

'The court reporter. He records everything anyone says.'

We crowded around a list on a wall called the Court calendar. There, at number seven in the list, was our case, 'Michael Carey v. Scott Brooks.' My name wasn't mentioned. Marcy motioned for Scott and me to sit in one of the wooden pews. The bench was very hard and uncomfortable. More and more people filed into the room, talking and carrying stacks of papers. Lawyers kept coming in and out of the room, some of them wheeling suitcase type bags filled with velobound bundles of paper. The atmosphere was different than I expected. It was quite calm. There was none of that resigned hopelessness in the air that made Family Court so horrible. I asked Marcy if I had time to go to the bathroom and she said yes, but to hurry up because the nearest ladies' bathroom was a long way away, two floors below.

I got a bit lost going to the bathroom and it was on my way back when I rounded the corner closest to our courtroom that I saw him. I only saw his back at first but the second I saw him, I knew who it was. He had the same shade of boot polish-black hair as I do except with streaks of grey at the temples. Michael turned around and saw me. It was super strange to see my own light grey eyes in his face. He looked like me or I looked like him, whatever. I felt mad that I looked like him and not like Mum; it felt like a betrayal of her in a weird way. He hesitated for a second and then he smiled tentatively at me. It was such a warm real kind of smile with crinkles at his eyes that I very nearly smiled back. But I pulled myself together and marched right past him with my head in the air. I hope he didn't notice that my left leg was shaking.

'Are you ok?' asked Scott when I returned.

I nodded.

'He's here,' I said.

Scott turned to look. Michael walked up the middle aisle of the courtroom past our pew, and stood near the top of the courtroom talking with his lawyer, Mr Tully. Michael didn't hire that guy based on his looks. Mr Tully was thin and scrawny with a face like a bat and an uncanny resemblance to Gollum. His loose, sloppy pinstriped suit hung off him as if he'd bought a size to match his ego instead of his body. He reeked of a very distinct oily cologne that hung in the air like incense.

Mr Tully said something to Michael. If a rat could talk, it would sound like him, wheedling and greedy and self-satisfied. Rob sat down beside Scott and me and told us that Mr Tully was a heavy hitter in the world of New York family law.

'He bills eight hundred dollars an hour,' said Rob.

'Nobody's worth that kind of money,' said Scott.

'You can tell he hates kids,' I piped up.

'You can tell he hates women,' said Marcy.

'That guy just hates people, period,' said Scott.

Marcy said that Mr Tully was the one 'driving' the case. I didn't say anything to that because well, Michael hired the guy.

The security guard said, 'All rise for the Honourable Justice Paul Hansen.' We stood up and an irritated looking small man with lank grey hair and thick glasses marched into the room as if he owned the place (which I suppose he kind of does) and sat at his desk. He raised his right hand in the air and waved it wearily at us as if we were his subjects.

'All sit,' boomed the security guard.

The judge leaned over his desk and began talking to the pretty blonde woman at the desk in front of him. She laughed politely at something he said. The clerk, a skinny black woman in a dishevelled black suit stood up and called out the names on the court calendar. When it came to our turn, the clerk said,

'Number seven on the calendar, Carey and Brooks.'

All the lawyers on the case stood up. Scott and I went to stand up as well, but Marcy motioned at us to remain sitting.

'For the petitioner, Michael Carey,' said Mr Tully.

'For the respondent, Dr Scott Brooks,' said Rob.

'For the child,' said Marcy.

Mr Tully began talking to the judge about some fundraiser they had both been at the week before. They seemed like good buddies. Scott shifted uncomfortably in his seat.

'Your Honour, I have a deposition in the Ordenez matter later today and I wonder if I might trouble you to take this case out of order,' asked Mr Tully.

'Certainly Mr Tully, I'm happy to accommodate your schedule,' said the Judge.

I'm not sure if I misheard the fleck of sarcasm.

'Lawyers only on Carey and Brooks,' said the judge. He didn't look at us. The judge and the three lawyers trooped through a door into a room behind the judge's desk. The door was left open a crack and we could hear the murmur of voices. There was a lot of laughter. I rigidly forced myself not to look at Michael sitting in a pew two rows in front and to the right of us although I could tell that he looked at me a lot. I shivered.

'Cold?' asked Scott.

I shook my head and he put his arm around me for a minute.

We waited for two thousand years for the lawyers to come out. Okay, it was more like half an hour but it felt like it took forever. The Judge came out first and returned to his chair and began looking through some papers on his desk. Marcy walked up to me, trailing pens and pieces of paper from her bulging briefcase onto the floor. I got up and picked them up.

'Ok,' she said breezily, 'let's go, we're done here.'

'What?' Scott and I said in unison.

'But nothing's happened,' added Scott. 'Isn't the Judge going to say something to us?'

Marcy shrugged. He's supposed to address the parties but usually he doesn't bother. It's more comfortable to deal just with the lawyers.

'More comfortable for whom?' snapped Scott.

'So what happened?' I asked.

'We talked about the status of the case,' said Rob. 'The Judge wants the forensics finished by the end of the month and he also scheduled a date for a pre-trial conference.'

Marcy interrupted. 'I have to leave. I have to be in Family Court in the Bronx, I'll call you,' and after kissing the air beside my cheek, she sailed off.

Scott turned to Rob. 'What a ridiculous waste of time! So

many lawyers here, most of whom seem to be getting paid by me, and for what?'

'I hear you,' said Rob, 'I understand your frustration. The wheels of justice grind slowly.'

'Grind slowly! That's an understatement. Nothing happened!'

Rob looked embarrassed.

'We have a date for the pretrial conference,' he pointed out.

'And it takes a judge and an army of lawyers to pick a date,' snapped Scott but then he ran his hand through his hair and added, 'Sorry, Rob, not your fault. This whole thing is driving me crazy. I'll talk to you tomorrow. Come on, Evie, let's go.'

We went out to the hallway and squeezed into the elevator. It stopped on the floor below. An old man used his cane to shove his way inside the already packed elevator. Seeing Scott, he announced:

'Jax didn't make it Doctor.'

'Umm, I'm sorry to hear that,' said Scott.

Everyone in the elevator perked up their ears.

'He was only three years old. He should have had a long life in front of him,' said the old man sadly.

A hum of sympathetic mutterings fluttered around the elevator. A plump, middle-aged woman pulled a tissue out of her handbag and wiped her eyes.

'You misdiagnosed it, Doc,' the old man added.

'I did?' said Scott. I could tell he was scrambling frantically around his brain, trying to remember who this old man was and who Jax was.

He had a stab at it.

'Um, did you bring Jax into the clinic last fall?' he asked.

'Last Fall? I brought him in two years ago to see you and he died three days later! He was a son to me,' said the old man contemptuously, waving his cane in the air with such force that it knocked off one of the passenger's dangling silver earrings. I bent down to pick it up but a young man in a grey suit stepped on it and it shattered into little pieces.

Everyone, except the woman, who had had the earring ripped from her ear, was now staring disapprovingly at Scott and shaking their heads.

'Here's my card,' said the man in the grey suit to the old man. 'I'm a lawyer. You might be entitled to compensation for medical negligence.'

'Thank you,' said the old man, putting the business card in his pocket.

We reached the ground floor and all the passengers streamed out.

'Was Jax your cat?' Scot asked the old man.

'A cat!' said the old man in a highly insulted tone. 'Odious cold creatures. My Jax was the most affectionate pet I ever had, the star of my snail farm. He was destined for great things.'

'Do you people hear that? Jax was a SNAIL!' shouted Scott at the crowd heading out the main doors but they had already moved on with their lives.

'A snail,' he repeated shaking his head.

'Scott, you might want to let it go now,' I suggested gently, taking him by the arm.

It was a lousy day all round.

# Chapter 16

When Scott and my mum were kids, they spent most of their summers with their parents at a cabin in the woods close to Highland Lake. Mum often talked about those family vacations, but my geography was pretty bad then (and not much better now), and I assumed that anything with the name 'Highland' must be in Scotland. In fact, Highland Lake is near a town called Winsted in northern Connecticut and it takes two hours and twenty-five minutes of fast driving to get there from our apartment on the Upper West Side. The reason I know this is that Scott took me, Kylie, Greg, Lorcan and Ben there this past weekend in his old Jeep. Lorcan was a last minute add-on after I begged Scott to invite him. Scott said Lorcan is too cocky. Joanna thinks that is ironic coming from Scott. Anyway, I thought Scott would like Lorcan if he got the chance to know him better. Scott thinks Lorcan is a bit phony. He said that Lorcan pretends to act like an adult.

I told Scott, "That's not Lorcan pretending. That *is* Lorcan.'

Joanna rather reluctantly agreed to take care of my bird Persie for the weekend. I owe her *big time*.

The wood cabin was built in the 1860s to store ice. During

the Second World War, someone converted it into a place to live. It sits alone at the bottom of a little steep hill backing into the woods. It was dark when we arrived and the Jeep got stuck in a swampy mixture of snow and mud, which put Scott into a dark mood. But by using our combined weight, we managed to heave it out of the mud, only narrowly missing running Ben over. (Greg was steering).

The trees are so close to the cabin that when the wind blows hard, the branches tap against the windows. It wasn't a scary ghostly noise. It sounded like the trees reminding us that they were there, but Lorcan didn't like it. He said it was weird and creepy and he'd prefer the sound of taxi horns any night of the week. Lorcan has an urban soul.

There are two small rather musty bedrooms downstairs and a huge loft upstairs that can only be reached by climbing a wide wooden plank ladder. Kylie and I shared the loft. Ben drove us all crazy with his barking because he couldn't climb the ladder. Greg spent ages on Friday night constructing a rope pulley system with a basin so we could haul Ben up and down. But when we tried to put Ben in the basin, he ran out the front door of the cabin and we didn't see him again for two hours.

Scott made a really big deal in the car on the way up here about how we were going to have a TV and gadget free weekend, the whole back-to-nature thing. We didn't care so much about the TV but were definitely a bit freaked out by the thought of not having wi-fi. As it turned out, the summer tenants had left a TV in the cabin. Right after we arrived, Scott spent two and a half hours trying to make the TV work, without success.

To me, America has always meant the skyscrapers of New York. I thought of the countryside as being something far away in the past, like Huckleberry Finn, but, Highland Lake is as rural as anywhere in the west of Ireland. There are no street lights and the closest neighbors are down by the lake except for Chet, an old man who lives in a nearby hut with Skully, his ginormous dog of indeterminate breed, a 52-inch plasma screen that is bigger than his bathroom, piles and piles of dusty issues of *National Geographic* magazine and a stock-pile of cans of tuna to tide him over if he is snowed in.

Skully is probably the friendliest dog in the world – at least that's what Kylie said when, in his enthusiasm about greeting visitors, he knocked her to the floor with his rudder-like tail. Lorcan said,

'That's not a dog, it's a bear.'

I think Skully might be part-bear. Scott told us that there are real hibernating bears out there in the woods, but that seemed about as real to me as Yogi-Bear. We don't have any remotely potentially frightening animals in Ireland. The only thing you have to be wary of when walking in the woods are the nettles.

We had a lot of fun over the weekend. We skated on the frozen lake and later, we hiked the trails in the woods. We were all impressed that Greg could name so many of the different types of trees. He was modest, like he always is.

'Finn taught me,' he said. 'It's like he was born knowing

that kind of stuff. My mom, I mean, my birth mom back in Wisconsin, used to say that I was born with a pencil in my hand and Finn was born with an axe.'

Greg sounded a little wistful as he said this as if he wished he was more like Finn.

'I think that you and Finn were both born with a pencil and an axe,' said Kylie, who always wants her friends to feel good about ourselves. She was about to say something else, but Lorcan interrupted her.

'When I was born, I was immediately wrapped in a cashmere blanket. I wish I had that blanket now. It is insanely freezing out here. Let's haul it back to the cabin.'

On Sunday morning, Scott pulled out his old sledge from underneath the cabin and suggested we go sleighing in nearby Burr Pond State Park. The sleigh was simple and light, made of wood and painted fire engine red. The paint had hardly peeled at all but Lorcan laughed when he saw it, and said it was a relic from the twentieth century.

'So am I,' said Scott, 'a relic from the twentieth century. Feel free to stay behind.'

'I'll do that,' said Lorcan smoothly, 'I have some stuff to take care of.'

'Great,' snapped Scott.

I wished Scott and Lorcan got on together better. They have a persistent knack for rubbing each other up the wrong way.

Closing my eyes, I ran my hand along the smooth warm nutty brown wood of the sleigh. For a brief moment, I could picture Mum and Scott as children sitting on the sleigh, Scott in front, her behind, clutching tightly to him, her long blonde hair streaming in the wind from under her yellow bobble hat. They were screaming with laughter.

'I love this old sleigh,' I said, 'it's perfect.'

Later, as Kylie and I hurtled down a hill, we laughed hysterically with the whole wonderful whishing joy of it all, the sleet lightly spraying our faces, the roaring muffled sound of the wind in our ears and the blue tinged sparkles of the freshly fallen snow. I thought Lorcan was crazy to miss this. On our second last run of the day, the runners hit a hidden stone, tipping the sleigh so we landed in a heap, headfirst in a snow bank, screaming like crazy, with arms and legs flailing.

'Wow, that felt like flying,' I gulped, spitting a hard lump of icy snow out of my mouth.

'The way an ostrich would fly,' said Kylie.

'I thought ostriches couldn't fly,' I said.

'Exactly,' said Kylie, carefully dusting snow powder from her bomber jacket. I marveled at how her hat still sat perfectly jauntily on her head.

'I can't believe your hat didn't even fall off,' I said picking icy particles embedded in my hair.

'Akono gave me this hat,' she said in what I would call a meaningful voice.

I stared at her. Why would Akono give her a hat? That didn't make any sense. She looked back at me.

'We're kind of going out now.'

'OMG,' I said, 'Greg was right! Why didn't you tell me?

And, I can't believe this, I mean what about your preparation for your career, you know, the sacrifices you have to make.'

'Akono isn't going to interfere with any of that. He's very supportive of my goals,' Kylie assured me. 'Aren't you happy for me? Don't you like him?' and she looked disappointed.

'Yes, of course I like him. Akono's great,' I stuttered, 'I'm just surprised. Why didn't you tell me?'

'It just sort of happened,' said Kylie 'and I was kind of embarrassed because I've always said that I wouldn't waste my time on boys and I didn't want you to feel left out because I have a boyfriend now. Nothing is going to change!'

It will change, I thought. It already has. But I said,

'Of course not,' and I hugged her, 'I'm happy for you silly,' I said.

'I knew you would be,' she said. 'I'm still kind of surprised myself. Akono is *so* not my type. But he's very persistent and he does the cutest thing when he is distracted, he puts one hand behind his back, like this,' and she demonstrated, giggling a little. Hmm, I didn't really get what was cute about it but I smiled enthusiastically.

'You have to get a boyfriend too so the four of us can hang out together,' said Kylie, 'oh, and with Greg of course.'

'A boyfriend! Scott would have a total meltdown. He thinks that I will be ready to start exploring romantic relationships when I'm THIRTY,' and I pulled a face.

Kylie laughed as we trudged back up the hill pulling the sleigh behind us.

'I miss Akono sooooo much,' she said wistfully.

We had only been gone for two days. People in *like* need a little indulging, I realised.

# Chapter 17

That night, our last night at Highland Lake, Scott hooked up some outside heaters so we could have supper outside on the side porch under the stars. He even fired up the BBQ. Eating hamburgers outside with snow on the ground and the dark shadows of the trees was a pretty special experience. After we ate, I cleared up the table outside as everyone else went inside to help with the washing up. As I picked up a plate of pickles, I heard frantic hysterical barking. Ben shot out the door onto the porch, foam dripping down the sides of his mouth as he stared at something behind me. I'd never seen Ben like that before. Puzzled, I turned swiftly around. There, almost within touching distance, stood a gigantic brown bear on its hind legs, looking at me. I'd seen bears before in zoos of course but there's a universe of difference between an animal the size of small car, behind iron bars and one out in the wild, with supper on his mind. He didn't look cute or cuddly or friendly. He looked ... REAL.

I froze, rooted to the floorboard as if my legs were encased in cement, the plate of pickles still in my hand. Ben's hoarse barking felt like it was coming from a long distance away.

It was only later I learned that everything I did was wrong. I stared back at the bear, looking directly into his black eyes. What I should have done was wave my arms up and down to try and make myself look as big as possible while avoiding making eye contact. To say that I felt *frightened* is woefully inadequate. I felt terror unlike anything I'd ever experienced before, a primal fear of being eaten alive, like a prehistoric cave girl.

Ben's barking attracted attention and Scott strolled out onto the porch and came to an abrupt stop. In a low, quiet, calm voice, he said,

'Evie, go into the cabin. Don't run.'

I have no idea how long I had been standing there, the bear and me, looking at one another. But Scott's comforting voice penetrated through the layer of sludge that seemed to be wrapped around my brain. Bending down, I grabbed hold of Ben by his collar and dragged him with me into the cabin. Scott was right behind me. The sound of the bolt on the lock sliding home, was one of the sweetest sounds I have ever heard.

'What's going on?' asked Kylie.

'Bear,' I said, but no actual sound came out of my mouth. I pointed out the window, where the bright porch light illuminated the great big shadow of the bear.

'Aaaaaaaaggggggggggggggggggggggggggg,' screamed Kylie.

We all jumped. The bear seemed irritated by the noise. It got down on all four paws and began to circle the cabin. We followed his progress through the windows, Ben still barking like crazy and Kylie, screaming like crazier.

Scott picked up his cell phone and called the local police.

A law enforcement clerk called Mary answered. I didn't catch her last name. Scott gave our address and explained that there was a very large bear outside the cabin.

'Nuffin' we can do,' said Mary in a bored voice as if he had reported that the toilet was leaking.

'But I have kids here at the cabin,' Scott said.

'We can't do anything,' repeated Mary, 'not unless the bear is actually attacking you. Is the bear attacking any of you right now?'

'Is that a joke?' asked Scott.

'No,' Mary said in an offended voice, 'like I said, unless the bear is attacking, we can't do anything. Has it got an orange tag because the bears that have been in trouble before, we tag them.'

'No, no tag,' said Scott.

'Well that's good,' said Mary, 'that means he ain't been in no trouble before.'

'Great,' said Scott, 'I hope the bear remembers that.'

'You can't shoot him,' said Mary, 'It's illegal in the state of Connecticut.'

'Of course I'm not going to shoot that magnificent animal,' said Scott in an exasperated voice, 'I thought that if you spotted a bear in a residential area, particularly where there are kids and dogs around, you need to report it to the local authorities, which is what I'm doing.'

'The right thing to do,' confirmed Mary sounding

friendlier. After a final reminder to call her back if the bear attacked, she hung up. We continued to watch the bear through the window. Ben climbed up on the top of the couch to get a better look, still barking so loudly in a way that frayed on the nerves. His poor legs were trembling like jelly. I gave him a hug to thank him for warning me about the bear.

The bear lay down on the grass in front of the cabin and rolled around. He didn't look so dangerous now. Then he got up, yawned, ambled up the hill and we could see the dark shadowy outline making his way slowly down the road towards the lake. After he had gone, we started to laugh. I don't know who started it but it was pretty hard to stop.

Even though Scott told us we were perfectly safe inside, when we all went to bed, Lorcan took a knife from the kitchen with him for extra security. I couldn't imagine plunging a knife into any animal. I selected a large frying pan and stowed it under my bed. Ben had ceased barking at last. I fell asleep to the comforting sound of his loud snores reverberating through the cabin.

It felt like only seconds later that Scott was shaking me awake, telling me to jump to it, that it was five in the morning. We needed to leave early to be at school in time. Everyone hustled around the cabin gathering up their stuff wordlessly. It was too early to speak. Right before we left, Scott picked up a framed photograph from the mantelpiece, stared at it for a few minutes before putting it back down. It was a photograph of his parents and him and Mum eating in the porch on a sunny day, back when Mum was about my age now. I never got to meet my grandparents. They died in a car crash the year I was born. They hadn't even known they had a granddaughter. Everyone in that photograph was gone now except for Scott. That weekend for the first time in a long time, I hadn't thought about anything to do with the custody case but suddenly I felt a surge of pure rage from deep in my belly at Michael for suing Scott for custody. Ben and me; we were all that Scott had left.

'Evie,' called Scott from the door, 'what are you doing hanging around? Everyone else is in the car. Let's go.'

'Coming,' I said, and I put the photograph down. I'm not going to let Michael separate Scott and me. Never. Not in a zillion years!

# Chapter 18

My lawyer, Marcy, called a few days ago to tell me I had an appointment with a psychologist for a *forensic* evaluation. She kept referring to the *forensics*. The only forensics I know about are from TV cop shows. Marcy said that Michael's lawyer, Mr Tully, had hired a 'big gun,' in the weird world of forensic child psychologists. His name, she said, was Dr Austin Blakely. Marcy sounded annoyed, but not surprised. She said that usually the court appoints one psychologist, called a 'Neutral', and that's it. But the parties in the case have the right to each get their own psychologist. That's what Michael's lawyer had done by hiring Dr Blakely. Marcy sighed and said that now we would have to hire our own psychologist too.

'That's ridiculous,' I said. 'This whole thing keeps getting worse and worse.'

'Don't worry,' said Marcy.

Huh. That was easy for her to say. It wasn't *her* family that had to face THREE shrinks.

'I know someone we can get who is cheap,' said Marcy. 'Her name is MaryAnn. She'll love Scott … oh, and you.'

I wish I had one of those lawyers on TV, the kind who

inspire confidence.

The following day, Scott and I went round to the big Barnes and Noble on Broadway and flicked through a book, *Co-Parenting Using the Austin Blakely Method*.™ There was an enormous photograph of Dr Blakely on the back dust jacket of the book. In it, he is sitting in a beige leather armchair surrounded by a group of remarkably photogenic children. He is smiling confidently into the camera. He looked young and tanned, the type of person who does six marathons a year and always remembers to floss. He had a thick mane of tawny golden brown hair and a dimple in his chin.

Dr Blakely's office is on a high floor in a very posh building on Park Avenue. All of the other doctors on his floor were cosmetic surgeons. Even though we arrived on time for the appointment, Scott and I had to wait nearly half an hour, which was particularly boring because the only reading materials in the waiting room were copies of Dr Blakely's books. Finally, his administrative assistant announced that Dr Blakely was ready to see us. She said it like we were about to meet a President of the United States, one of the really good ones whose name everyone can remember.

There was only a faint resemblance between the man in the dust jacket photograph and the real live Dr Blakely. He looked about twenty years older and his hair was very thin with the faint greenish tinge of dubious highlights, nothing like the thick mane of tawny hair in the photo. He also looked a lot shorter, although to be fair, he was sitting down in the photo. There was no trace of a dimple. I suppose that had been photoshopped in.

Dr Blakely's office was filled with beige leather furniture and paintings (not the kind you buy on eBay). In one corner, there was a montage of brightly-coloured 'thank you' letters from his clients. He stood up as we entered his office.

'Evangeline, Jock, I'm so happy to be working with you,' he said in a jovial but surprisingly reedy voice, 'call me Dr Blakely.'

'Call me Scott,' said Scott as he shook hands. As Dr Blakely shook my hand, I noticed his perfectly-manicured square nails.

'We're not exactly working with you,' Scott pointed out, 'Evie's biological dad hired you and we don't have any choice but to go along with this crazy process.'

Dr Blakely immediately put on an expression of such sympathetic understanding and concern that I felt squeamish. He was a big phony. Even the average two-year-old would have been able to sense that.

Our meeting lasted exactly forty-three minutes. It was supposed to last an hour so Dr Blakely must be ripping Michael off. That didn't bother me. Dr Blakely spent most of the time talking about himself and discreetly checking his large gold watch. He explained that he had started his career as a highly-successful executive in Boston. He was sketchy about what that actually involved. He told us that his life lacking meaning and purpose – he wanted to find some way to contribute to the world, to be a force for positive change and to make a difference in the lives of children of parents in conflict. He spent years devising the Austin Blakely Co-Parenting Method. Yawn. I'm just summing it up here. The method seems to involve ticking off checklists using special colour coded highlighters. You get a free pack of highlighters when you buy your first Dr Blakely book and a fifteen percent discount off the second book.

He didn't ask Scott or me any questions. He emphasised that he mainly works with divorcing celebrities and sports stars and their children but that he made room in his hectic schedule to take on this case. He paused at that point as if expecting us to thank him. When we didn't say anything, he looked a little disappointed.

'Do you have any questions for me?' he asked at last.

I could tell from Scott's face that he was struggling to resist the temptation to slide in a snide comment. Marcy had told me that it is very important to be pleasant at all times with the forensics. To try and stall Scott from being sarcastic, I asked Dr Blakely,

'Where is the loo?' (It was the only question I could think of under pressure).

Dr Blakely looked faintly annoyed and suggested that I hang on because we were nearly finished – he had to catch the red-eye to LA to meet with a very dear friend of his, a famous actress, who was involved in a highly contentious divorce. He told us her name in a hushed reverent voice. She couldn't be that famous because neither Scott nor I had ever heard of her.

As we were leaving, Dr Blakely insisted on presenting

us with one of his books. Two days later, Scott received an invoice in the mail from Dr Blakely's office, charging him for the book. I thought he was going to freak out but he didn't say a single word. He picked up that invoice, crumpled it into a ball and threw it into the plastic basin I had converted into a toilet for Persie. It was a perfect shot.

# Chapter 19

The next forensic psychologist on the list was Marcy's MaryAnn Something. I couldn't muster much enthusiasm about meeting another member of *Team Marcy*, but tried to have a good attitude about it. MaryAnn's office was in the reddish Lipstick Building on 53rd Street and Third. From the outside, it looks like open tube of lipstick. Inside, it's just an ordinary office building, and pretty shabby compared to Dr Blakely's offices.

MaryAnn was a tall, skinny, black woman from New Jersey with a dark hairy mole to the right of her nose. It was incredibly difficult to avoid looking at the mole. She wore a tight-fitting suit with a pencil skirt in a tired shade of red. Having seen her knees, I will never complain about mine being knobby again.

MaryAnn didn't shortchange us on time. Far from it. Escaping from her was no easy feat. Unlike Dr Blakely, she asked a ton of questions, but they were all addressed to Scott and they all concerned one thing – Scott's romantic history. I might as well have been invisible. Poor Scott, the way he lightly dodged around her questions reminded me of an impala I'd seen on the Discovery Channel.

Scott tried to divert the conversation to me. He didn't succeed but at least he got MaryAnn off the topic of his love life and on to her own. She told a long story about her divorce. It was funny in parts, but not that funny. I don't think I was supposed to feel sorry for her ex-husband. When the story finished, she sighed and said to Scott in an embarrassing little girl voice, 'It is extremely difficult for black professional women in New York to date.'

Scott replied nonchalantly that it was very difficult for everyone in New York to date.

I added (helpfully, I thought), 'My friend Akono's mom is black and she's a doctor and she didn't have any problem in dating his dad. They're very happily married now. Well, I assume they're happy. Akono never—'

MaryAnn cut me off with a snarl. Scott looked a little scared. I don't know if that was because of the snarl or because by this time, MaryAnn had maneuvered herself so that she was practically sitting in his lap.

He was saved by Mr Fannelli who called to say that Spike had eaten a large tub of hot chili stuffed olives and was acting a little funny.

Scott answered, 'If I ate a whole tub of hot chili stuffed olives, I'd be acting a little funny too. I'll be there in twenty minutes.'

'Emergency, I have to go,' he said to MaryAnn.

She pouted, which seemed to magnify the size of her mole. She gave Scott her business card, on which she wrote her personal cell number and asked him to call her. I had a feeling that card would also make it to Persie's pooping basin. As we struggled to get past her to the door, she handed me a questionnaire to fill out. It was very long, about thirty pages, and, asked loads of questions like, 'What do I typically eat for breakfast?' and 'How many hours per week do I spend playing computer games?'

The following day, just as the Spanish teacher walked in, I passed the questionnaire to Greg. He loves a writing project. It took him the next three classes to fill it out. When school finished for the day, Kylie and I read his answers. Wow. Greg is an amazing writer with a fantastic imagination. He did a great job although I don't think he should have written that Scott and I pray together every night and well, lots of other stuff as well. Greg can be a bit touchy about his writing. I tried to be sensitive in suggesting that he maybe change it a bit to stick much closer to the truth. He took that pretty well. He said he would take out all the blatant lies, leaving me wondering what kind of lies he was going to leave in. But I didn't have much time to worry about it because I had yet another forensic psychologist to visit at five o'clock.

The third and final psychologist I had to see, Marcy called the 'Neutral,' because it was the psychologist appointed by the Court. She was a young, pretty Hispanic woman, named Rosita. She asked to meet me by myself in a Starbucks. She smiled at me in a warm, sincere way. Her eyes were infused with that fleck of intense light that let me know straight away that she had a sense of humour. She also looked like she hadn't slept in several years. I suppose that's why she needed the triple espresso. She asked me lots of questions, but not in an intrusive way, she seemed to just slip them in naturally as part of the conversation. Every now and then, she would scribble something in her lined, yellow legal pad. Mainly, she just listened and smiled or laughed now and again. When we talked about my mum dying, she was so genuinely sympathetic that I wondered if her own mom had died. Eventually, she closed her notebook and said,

'Evie, you seem like a happy well-adjusted kid, especially given how short a time it has been since your mom's death. The credit for how well you're doing has to go to you and to your uncle Scott and that's what I will tell the Judge in my report.'

'Thank you,' I said.

'Thank *you*,' she said with a smile and before we left, she bought herself another espresso to go.

# Chapter 20

I love amusement parks (who doesn't) and so on Saturday morning, when Lorcan suggested we take a trip out to Coney Island, I was totally up for it. I immediately said I would text Kylie and Greg, oh and better include Akono too, but Lorcan wasn't enthusiastic.

'I'm not in the mood for a crowd. Let's go by ourselves … a bit of spontaneity.'

'I'm up for some spontaneous spontaneity,' I answered into the phone, unintentionally showering Ben's head with saliva. He waggled his long floppy ears. It was impressive. Kylie can waggle her left ear. I can't make either of my ears move even a centimeter. I appreciate this inability is unlikely to hamper my prospects in life but still, it would be nice to have that extra skill. Kylie said I should be grateful I have nice nail beds. Seriously. How useless is that? I didn't even know nails had beds. And what do nasty nail beds look like anyway?

'Evie, are you still there?' asked Lorcan.

'Yeah, sorry,' I said, 'just thinking. I'll meet you at half-ten.'

I didn't admit to Lorcan that there is absolutely *no way* Scott would let me go all the way out to Coney Island in Brooklyn without adult supervision. Lorcan wouldn't understand.

He might even feel sorry for me. His dads are pretty fantastic about treating him like a grown-up. If they are thinking about doing something, they ask him very courteously, 'does that fit in with your schedule, Lorcan?' Nobody has ever asked me about consulting my 'schedule.'

Happily, Scott was away all day, judging a dog agility competition somewhere in the wilds of Pennsylvania. Nobody offered to accompany him except me but Scott said I had to stay at home and concentrate on reading American books. It's a long story – last week, when Scott came by school to pick me up, Mrs Billington, my very proper and boring English teacher, cornered us at the gate. She told Scott that I was being stubborn about using the Queen's English instead of US English. She said that in a terrible, cringe-worthy fake British accent and then she laughed as if she had said something hysterically funny. After a split-second pause, Scott laughed politely along with her. I said, with a perfectly straight face, 'I'm most awfully sorry Mrs Billington. I will try my jolly best to spiff up my spelling.' Scott poked me very hard in my back and marched me out to his Jeep, which was illegally parked by the way.

'It's a respect issue,' said Scott, 'you didn't show respect for your teacher and that's not cool.'

'Well,' I sniffed, 'it's not particularly respectful to *me* that she can't remember I'm Irish, not British. And anyway, I never said anything disrespectful to her before. I swear I always fall asleep in her class as soon as she starts talking.'

I glanced sideways at Scott expecting him to laugh. But

he didn't.

'Because falling asleep in her class is the height of respect,' Scott said drily. 'Evie, not everything is a joke.'

I gawped at him, my mouth open. Scott was the High King of Not Taking Anything Overly Seriously.

'But … but …' I stuttered.

Scott cut in.

'Has it occurred to you Evie that Mrs Billington could be spending her precious time doing something much more entertaining and much better paid than trying to teach some ungrateful kids?'

'No,' I said feeling a red tsunami of shame washing over me.

Scott tousled my hair.

'Don't beat yourself up, at least, not too hard. Just give Mrs Billington a chance. Okay? At least she cares and is trying, which is a lot better than some of the teachers I had in school.'

'Ok,' I said.

'And why are you insisting on sticking to English English? Is this some of your Irish identification issues run wild?'

'No,' I said, 'I'm not remotely being stubborn about my spelling. Basically, you have to drop a lot of u's like, C-O-L-O-R not C-O-L-O-U-R. What do Americans have against the letter "u" anyway? My problem is when I'm writing, I often get confused about which is the American way and which is the English way.'

'Read more books written in American English, that will help,' suggested Scott.

Saturday had been set aside (by him, not by me) as my catch-up on reading American English books day. I figured I could just as easily do my extra reading on the subway out to Coney Island with Lorcan. There was only the teeny issue about getting permission to go. Scott would say 'dream on,' or something like that but luckily, he was out for the day watching assorted Labrador retrievers jump off specially constructed diving boards. Joanna was working in the clinic but I didn't consider asking her because she would just say, call Scott. I decided to ask Holly, who, after all, is an adult and is one of Scott's employees, which sort of gives her semi-legitimate agent-guardian type status. I found Holly slouched on the couch painting her toenails and watching back-to-back episodes of a TV show about people addicted to cosmetic surgery. Sometimes I watch it with her and we make a game of guessing which animal the patient will most closely resemble when they are done. Mostly, they end up looking like surprised geckos although one poor guy wound up looking like a warthog.

Holly's been hanging out in the apartment a lot lately because she hates having to commute in and out from Astoria to Manhattan. She's even here on her days off because she usually has to be in the city on those days to go to auditions. Scott, who would rather hack off one of his legs than commute, was sympathetic to Holly's plight. He gave her a key and told her she could hang out in the apartment whenever she wants. She's started to bring friends around recently, which Joanna told me was pushing it but then she sighed and said, 'Hey, none of my business!'

I was lucky Holly was here today. I waited for the exact right moment in the TV program.

'Hi Hol, is it ok with you if I go to Coney Island with Lorcan?' I chanted quickly, timing my request perfectly to coincide with when the doctor was about to remove the woman's bandages from her face.

'Um, sure Evie,' said Holly, without taking her eyes from the screen.

'Bye,' I said.

Lorcan and I took the D train. I think it was the oldest and slowest subway I have ever ridden but Lorcan talked the whole way so the trip went quickly. I decided to do my extra reading on the return journey. When we got to our stop and walked out of the subway station, we took a shortcut across two large deserted fenced-in parking lots. There wasn't anything but litter blowing around. I could see all the rides and the roller coasters in the distance. I wanted to run but Lorcan's too cool to run.

It was only when we got closer to the amusement park that we realised it was shut, closed down for the winter. The abandoned rides looked old and lonely and broken. The whole place looked eerie, not as if it was just sleeping but as if it had committed suicide. I shivered.

'Come on, we'll go walk on the boardwalk, you're freezing,' said Lorcan.

'Ok,' I said, not a bit sorry to leave that depressing place behind.

I had never been on a boardwalk before. It was a bit of a disappointment as well. It was just a long, wide, greyish path and all the little stores and amusement arcades along it were closed except for a hot dog stand. We bought some hot dogs to help us warm up and walked for what must have been miles along the boardwalk. The tide was quite far out and the dirty sand on the beach looked like cigarette ash. We could hear people speaking in Russian all around us, which made the place seem foreign and the right kind of dangerous. Well, I thought they were speaking Russian. Lorcan said it was Polish but he was wrong. There were a few Polish kids in my class at school in Ireland and I'm certain that the walkers on the boardwalk were not speaking Polish. That's when it happened, when I was arguing that the people were definitely not Polish. Lorcan tugged me closer to him by the cord on my hood and kissed me, very quickly. I'm so glad my first kiss was spontaneous. My second kiss was spontaneous as well. And the third. We went under the boardwalk and sat on the dry, quite smelly, sand and did lots more kissing, for about an hour. Turning thirteen had been so disappointing. My first kissing experience was brilliant. I felt like a different person, an older, more interesting person. I could kiss all the time.

On the way home on the subway, we sat quite close together in the two seats by the doors. An empty coke bottle floated in a small puddle on the floor in front of us. From the smell, I think it was pee. Lorcan sat on my left. I completely forget about my extra reading probably because I was entirely focused on what to do with my left hand. I didn't know where to put it. If I put it by my side like normal, Lorcan might think I expected him to hold it.

So, I folded my arms but he said, 'What's up with you?'

I said 'nothing' and I unfolded them.

But I still had the problem of what to do with my left hand. Finally, I sat on my hands. It just seemed the easiest thing to do. Then, Lorcan asked me if my hands were cold so I said no, and pulled them out again. We started talking about a concert in Madison Square Garden his dads have tickets for and he asked me if I wanted to go and we were so busy talking it took me a couple of minutes to realise Lorcan had taken my hand. Or maybe I took his, I'm not sure. It felt very special and grown-up to be holding hands with a boy on the subway although I had a weird passing fear that one of the other passengers would shout, 'Look, They're Holding Hands! Stop Them!'

I wished the ride would go on for the rest of the day and all night, but after a little while, I wished that it would end as soon as possible because I could feel my hand getting all sweaty and I didn't want to have to pull it away and wipe it on my coat. I thought about asking Lorcan to swap places with me because usually, it's just my left hand that gets sweaty. But I thought that would only draw more attention to the sweat.

Ultimately, it was a bit of a relief when we arrived back in Manhattan. Lorcan dropped my hand very naturally when we got off. I hope that wasn't because of the sweat.

Scott was home watching TV with Ben when I got home.

It was some championship poker game in Vegas so he was too distracted to ask me questions about my day. He always wears dark sunglasses when he watches poker. I think it makes him feel more involved in the game because most of the players wear glasses to hide their eyes.

He glanced at me and I thought he would notice straight away how different I was, like the evidence that I had been kissing a boy would be marked on my forehead like Harry Potter's scar. But Scott didn't seem to see anything. Then again, he was wearing sunglasses indoors and probably couldn't see much. He sneezed twice very loudly. He must have caught a cold watching dogs jump around outside all day. I felt this huge swell of love and affection for him, for spending a lousy day out in the middle of nowhere giving dogs marks for jumping just so he could add more money to our legal defense fund. I immediately offered that he could pick the restaurant on seamless web that we would order from. He said he wasn't in the mood for eating.

I slipped out to Zabars and bought Scott an extra-large tub of chicken noodle soup. He was so appreciative and nice about it, I felt a little guilty for not telling him that my relationship with Lorcan had shifted dramatically from friends to . . . well, whatever we were now. I got over the guilt rapidly by reassuring myself that it would only make him mad and it would be unhealthy for him to get all wound up when he's already sick. Besides, the right to privacy is enshrined in the Constitution. I did learn some things at school.

# Chapter 21

I've spent a little time thinking about whether I am Lorcan's girlfriend. I've spent even more time discussing the issue with Kylie and Greg. As far as Greg is concerned, it's a no-brainer; the rule of three; Lorcan and I are definitely boyfriend/girlfriend because we have now kissed on three separate occasions. But Kylie insists that I can't be Lorcan's girlfriend unless he's asked me to be his girlfriend.

'Or you've asked him,' she added hastily, 'it's not like girls have to sit around anymore waiting for some guy to make up his mind.'

Lorcan and I have never talked about anything remotely along those lines. But like me, he's Irish and we're not as upfront about discussing these kinds of things as Americans. I decided to consult Joanna because she's had lots of boy-friends (all whack-jobs according to Scott but he's biased).

I regretted talking to Joanna almost immediately because she got a bit soppy when I told her I was kissing a boy. She sighed and said I was growing up so fast, and, she didn't kiss her first boy until three days after her fifteenth birthday but kids, and everything else, move much faster nowadays, and, how I shouldn't feel pressured by the media or from my peers to grow up too fast, all that kind of thing. I was a little confused because at first, I thought she said 'pears' and I couldn't understand what fruit had to do with anything but then I copped on. I tried to be patient. When that failed, I concentrated on trying to look patient.

When I finally managed to persuade Joanna to focus on the issue of whether I *was or was* not Lorcan's girlfriend, she thought about it for a few minutes and said,

'Evie, you're asking the wrong question.'

I hate when people say stuff like that. It's plain annoying.

'What *is* the right question?' I sighed.

Joanna tried not to look smug.

'The question is not whether you *are* or are *not* Lorcan's girlfriend. The question is do you want to be his girlfriend?'

That stumped me.

'Em, I like the kissing part a lot,' I said.

'Too much information,' she said. 'It's simple. Do you want to be with Lorcan?'

'I don't know,' I said, feeling exceptionally stupid, 'I haven't really thought about that.'

'Maybe you should,' said Joanna kindly.

# Chapter 22

I was so excited for Finn that I couldn't swallow anything but half a banana for breakfast. Today was the day of his championship hockey game, being played in Madison Square Garden, just like the pros. Greg said that there would almost certainly be talent scouts at the game and that this could be Finn's big chance, the break of a LIFE-TIME.

I wasn't holding a grudge against Finn for just replying 'k' in response to my very genuine apology. Holly had helped. She told me that when Finn said 'ok', he probably meant exactly that and I was thinking too much. I've been accused of overthinking before so I thought Holly made sense. She ruined it a little by adding, 'Evie, think less, wear more make-up.'

Almost everyone I know came to the game, except Scott who was still in bed with what he says is the flu and what Joanna calls a trifling little cold. Dr Winters didn't come either. Greg told me that Finn and his dad argue all the time because Dr Winters thinks Finn is loaded with brains and he should go to college to be a doctor or a lawyer and not waste his time skating around on ice with a load of bar-

barians, carrying sticks. At least Finn's mom supports him. Angela sat beside us in the very front row along with loads of her eccentric, multiple-scarf-wearing friends. They annoyed Greg a lot because none of them seemed to understand the rules of the game and they cheered very loudly at the wrong parts, like when the other team, the Omaha Warriors, scored.

I found the game so thrilling that when I wasn't jumping up and down cheering, I sat at the very edge of my seat. The teams were very closely matched, but almost right from the start, Finn's team stayed out in front mainly thanks to his superstar goals. Whenever Finn scored, Greg tried to start a Mexican wave but it only worked twice. It can be tricky to get the timing right. Coltan didn't help with getting a wave going because he refused to even budge from his seat. He's so not a team player. He didn't even bother to glance at us. His eyes never strayed from the ice. I never would have guessed he was such a big hockey fan.

It was close to half-time when the fight broke out. I don't know what caused it. One minute, we were all ineffectually doing a Mexican wave and the next, Finn and a very large, husky looking Nebraskan, were wrestling on the patch of ice right in front of us. The no-nonsense looking referee pulled them apart. He lectured them and made them shake hands. As Finn walked away, the big Nebraskan guy shouted something at him. Finn spun around, dropped his hockey stick and punched the guy in his face. A spray of blood, a cartoon-red colour, shot out from the guy's nose, splattering the clear, plastic guard in front of my eyes. Two of the Omaha

Warriors lunged at Finn. Pandemonium broke out as both teams jumped into the fray. Around me, the crowd stamped and cheered like bloodthirsty spectators at the gladiatorial games in ancient Rome. I stood there silently, transfixed by the Nebraskan blood dripping down the plastic shield.

The scuffle on the ice came to an end and the referee and some other official looking guy in a striped black and white t-shirt were watching Finn skate off the rink.

'What's happening?' I said tugging impatiently on Akono's sleeve.

'The referee sent Finn off.'

'Until the next half?'

'Nope, for the whole game, it's over for him,' said Akono glumly.

'Kylie, come on, let's get some air,' he said and took her hand. She raised her eyebrows at me and I nodded.

'See you later, Ky,' I said and my voice sounded steady and normal.

I watched Tamara walk down the steps and wait by the post beside the entrance to the tunnel leading to the changing rooms so she would be able to meet Finn as soon as he came back out. Greg and Coltan followed her. Even Coltan seemed affected by what we had witnessed on the ice. His always lightly-tanned face had a faint greenish tinge. Maybe he couldn't stand the sight of blood.

Lorcan took my hand and started talking about whether we should order some nachos. I was livid.

'Nachos! What are you talking about?' I snapped, tugging

my hand away sharply. 'Have you been in a different stadium on a different planet to the rest of us? Don't you get it? Finn's been sent off. It's a total freaking disaster. He must be killing himself.'

Lorcan looked peeved.

'Lighten up, Evie,' he said curtly, 'It's just a game. I'm hungry. I'm ordering nachos. If you didn't want any, a simple "no thank you" would have done it!'

'Sorry,' I said miserably.

Lorcan shrugged and called over the guy with the electronic beeper thing to take down his order.

'You sure you don't want any?' Lorcan asked me.

'I'm sure,' I said.

The second half of the game started, but I had zero interest in watching it. Finn's team fell hopelessly behind. Lorcan ate his nachos very noisily.

'You know,' he said, wiping bright orange plastic cheese from his mouth, 'Finn's team is going to lose now because of his temper. If I was on his team, I would *not* be impressed with that dude.'

I felt like giving Lorcan a slap and only restrained myself by sitting on both of my hands. The game was only five minutes away from the end. It was a slaughter. I couldn't bear to watch anymore. I went to the bathroom. As I dried my hands, I heard the blow of the final whistle and the loud grating party song over the loudspeakers. Outside the bathroom, in the corridor, I noticed a hunched figure a little ahead. FINN! He must have come out some back exit.

'Finn,' I called, 'Wait up!'

He stopped and turned, looked at me and waited. The right side of his face was messed up pretty bad. I bit my lip.

'Are you ok?' I asked inanely.

'I've felt better,' he said.

'I'm sorry,' I said.

'For what? You didn't do anything. That was all me out there on the ice, me and my dumbass temper.'

'I'm sorry,' I said again, 'because I know it's so much worse when you do it to yourself.'

'It is, isn't it,' he said, 'I'm no better than my mom's drug dealer. Letting that dumb guy provoke me. That was their plan and I walked straight into it, like they knew I would. I blew it Evie, my one shot and I threw it away like it meant nothing.'

'You'll get another shot at it,' I said confidently.

'This isn't some Hollywood movie,' he said, 'there won't be any other chances. There are plenty of guys out there who can play. You think any scout is going to take a chance on someone with a discipline problem.'

'So you'll show them that you don't have a problem; that you can keep it together.'

'I told you. There won't be another chance.'

'You'll make one!' I said confidently.

'Doubt it,' he said but he gave me that familiar half-grin.

'You can do it,' I said, 'you're brave; you beat the New York divorce courts by running off to Wisconsin. So, this should be a cinch.'

143

'You're the one who's brave,' he said, 'watching your mother die and then having to move to a whole new country.'

I stared at the ground embarrassed.

'Oh come on,' I said, 'I moved to New York, hardly a hardship, it's not like I had to go live in some hut without electricity in … in … Malawi.'

He laughed but then said, 'Owww, don't make me laugh, it hurts.'

'Walk with me out of here,' he added, and I fell into step beside him.

'What did the guy say? The Omaha guy that made you lose it?' I asked.

'I don't want to talk about it,' said Finn as we walked through the maze of corridors in the Garden, 'Let's talk about something else. Anything else.'

'Like what?' I asked.

'Like you and that Irish kid, Lorcan, what's going on with you two? Greg says you guys are going out.'

'No. Yes. I mean, probably,' I said.

Finn glared at me.

'You're way too young to be seeing anyone. I can't believe Scott's letting you.'

My mouth dropped open and I felt like a bag of baby snakes had been ripped opened in my stomach. I put my hand on my gut to try and quell the wriggling sensation.

'I'm thirteen,' I said stiffly, 'Scott doesn't know and he doesn't need to know. Where do you get off telling me what

I should or shouldn't be doing? You're only two years older than me, you … you misogynist!'

Finn laughed.

'Do you even know that that means?' he teased.

'Of course I do,' I said haughtily, thinking PLEASE, GOD, LET ME HAVE PRONOUNCED IT PROPERLY.

The truth was I only had a hazy notion of what it meant. Any time Kylie's Mom, Rachel, had a bad date, she called the guy a misogynist. So, it seemed appropriate.

Finn put both of his hands lightly on my shoulders and leaned towards me. His blood-streaked face was so very close to mine. For the briefest of moments I crazily thought he was going to kiss me but he just looked at me with those dark eyes and I looked back at him.

'FINN!' called out Tamara who had appeared at the other end of the corridor. Finn casually took his hands off my shoulders.

'Don't get your knickers in a knot Evie. Isn't that the expression you use?' and he grinned, 'you're such good friends with Greg, I guess I feel the need to look out for you … like a kid sister.'

I don't think there's anything in the world he could have said that would have hurt more.

'FINN' yelled Tamara again and she rushed up the corridor and flung her long pretty arms around him. Seriously, even her arms are pretty.

She touched the cut on his right cheek.

'Poor baby,' she said.

He swung his arm around her and said, 'See you 'round, Evie.'

They walked off together, looking like Tom Brady and Giselle after an old Super Bowl, and left me standing there watching them, feeling like crying.

I turned around. A few feet away from me stood Coltan, leaning up against a door, staring at me with a look of such pure unconcealed hatred on his face that I took an involuntary step backwards. Nobody has ever looked at me like that before, not Scott's old girlfriend, Leela, not even the bear. How long had had he been standing there, watching? I took another step backwards and Coltan smirked at me, his usual supercilious bored look on his face. I hesitated. Had I just imagined his murderous look?

Lorcan appeared behind him.

'There you are, Evie,' he said impatiently, 'How long does it take to go to the bathroom? I've been looking everywhere for you. Come on, Simon's going to take us for lunch at Serendipity. The nachos were just an appetizer.'

'Ok,' I said and walked towards him past Coltan. I sneaked a look at Coltan's face but it was still the same smirk with no hint of the hatred, I thought I'd seen. Maybe, I was being paranoid. I let Lorcan take my hand. His hand felt warm and comforting. As we made our way out of the Garden, he talked about this and that, and about nothing, and that was comforting as well … the familiar sound of his Irish accent. Lorcan and me; we get each other.

# Chapter 23

On Saturday morning Scott got an unexpected phone call.

'Hello, Dr Brooks here,' Scott said, swallowing a mouthful of Cap'n Crunch.

There was silence at the other end of the line. So Scott and I knew straight away that the caller must be Stan, one of the keepers at the Central Park Zoo. He's terribly shy about speaking on the phone (and about speaking in general), which makes communication a little tricky.

'Stan, is that you?' asked Scott in a gentle tone.

I could hear Stan clearing his throat.

Scott pushed his bowl of cereal away so he could concentrate better on the difficult task of extracting information from Stan.

'Which animal at the zoo are you calling about?' asked Scott.

After a few seconds of silence, during which I could almost feel Stan's efforts to build up the will to speak, he answered, 'Milly.'

Scott gestured at me but he didn't have to. I had already grabbed the purple folder we keep with the names and histories of all the animals at the Zoo. I ran my finger down the 'M's' until I came to Milly.

'Alpaca,' I whispered to Scott, 'Adult Female. From Peru. Oh. She's eleven and a half months pregnant.'

Scott nodded at me.

'Is Milly showing signs of labour?' asked Scott.

A low humming sound came across the line.

'Excuse me? said Scott.

'HUMMMMMMMMMMMMMMMMMMMMMMMM,' Stan hummed again, much louder this time.

'Oh, I got it, I'll meet you at the alpacas' enclosure in ten minutes,' said Scott hanging up.

I looked at Scott confused.

'Stan is imitating Milly,' Scott explained. 'Alpacas often hum when they are close to giving birth. Come on, let's get our stuff.'

In my excitement, I half-ran down the spiral staircase to the clinic, tripping over Ben's favourite orange ball on the third last step and sliding the rest of the way so I landed on the floor on my bum with a painful jolt.

Scott's head appeared at the top of the stairs.

'This isn't the time for sitting around on your backside Evie. Get to it.'

'I'm coming,' I yelled, glaring at Ben, who had retrieved his ball and was giving it a good lick as if to compensate it for the unpleasantness of coming into contact with my foot. I scrambled to my feet. I was about to see an alpaca give birth. Saturday mornings don't get much better than that.

Nearly ten minutes later, after jogging through the Park, Scott and I reached the zoo and found Stan waiting for us close to the alpacas' enclosure. The alpacas looked like wooly white sheep crossed with hump-less camels. As we reached the gate, a large alpaca made a high pitched braying noise. It sounded like – WARK WARK, WARK WARK. And as Scott opened the gate, the big alpaca lifted up his head and spat at him. A streak of green grassy bile flew through the air in an arc. Scott ducked like a prizefighter and the alpaca spit hit me smack in the middle of my face. 'Uuugh,' I gasped, 'it's in my nose. Gross.' There was a deep low shuddering sound like a troubled jet plane approaching landing. (It was only later that I realised that was Stan laughing. I'm glad I afforded him the opportunity for a good laugh.)

'I'm guessing the spitter is Daddy,' Scott said cheerfully.

Stan nodded. 'His name is Arturo.'

'Look at the dung piles, Evie, what's unusual about them?' Scott asked. I wiped some spit out of my right eye with my sleeve so I could get a clearer look.

'Um, some of them are super tidy and others are a bit of a disaster.'

'Exactly,' said Scott, 'the tidy dung heaps are made by the males. The female alpacas are like some teenage girls I know. They can't use the bathroom without leaving it a mess.'

'Ha, ha,' I muttered tonelessly.

Scott grinned.

'I've never seen an alpaca before,' I said. 'We don't have any in Ireland.'

'They come from the Andes,' said Scott, 'the great mountain range in South America. Alpacas hate being wet. They could never tolerate living somewhere as rainy as Ireland.'

We reached the part of the enclosure that Stan had fenced off for Milly's use. She was lying on her side, panting a little and looking tired. The rest of the herd gathered as close as they could to Milly's enclosure. This was going to be a birth with a large, curious audience.

After washing and disinfecting his right arm and hand with the help of Stan's pail of hot water and some soap, Scott examined Milly.

'I can feel the cria's nose and front feet,' he said, 'it's a little big – Milly's getting exhausted from the effort of straining. I'm going to see if I can help ease the cria out.'

Fifteen minutes later, Scott announced, 'it's a boy,' and picking the cria up, gently swung him upside down.

'To help drain the fluid,' he explained.

Milly made a series of joyful clicking sounds at her baby. The herd of alpacas joined in with a chorus of clicks to welcome the new arrival. Scott handed me a towel to wipe the new mother down.

'But don't wipe the head and bottom areas; it's important to keep Milly's scent for the little one to recognise.'

As I towelled Milly down, the cria found her mom's teats and began to suck happily. The herd of alpacas began to hum. I found myself joining in, but was quickly drowned out by Stan's impressively deep resonant hum. He's the *American Idol* of hummers.

# Chapter 24

After school on Monday, I went home with Kylie, supposedly to study together.

When I first started school, I found, to my surprise, that I was a little ahead of the class in math, but I'd been doing steadily worse on the math tests all year. Last Friday, my math teacher, Mr Papadopoulos, asked me to stay behind after class. I felt that familiar sinking feeling in my gut. As the rest of the class filed out, a few of my friends shot me empathetic smiles. I tried to smile back. That wasn't easy because I overheard Camille telling Lorcan how *sorry* she felt for me. I hate when people feel sorry for me. But a put-down dressed up as sympathy is even worse. If I was still a little kid, I probably would have pulled her hair.

Mr Papadopoulos got straight to the point.

'Evie, I'm very disappointed with your progress in math. You seem to be going backwards. Is there anything going on at home that's distracting you?'

'No,' I said.

Mr Papadopoulos looked sceptical.

'Nothing different at home? A divorce, a new sibling?'

'No,' I said, 'I live with my uncle. Everything's fine.'

Mr Papadopoulos continued to press.

'What about boys? Do you have a boyfriend?'

'No,' I said quickly. It was so embarrassing to be talking about boys with Mr Papadopoulos. And even if Lorcan was my boyfriend, which I hadn't quite figured out yet, I couldn't see how that could possibly be any of Mr Papadopoulos's business. How would he like if I asked him if he had a wife or a husband?)

'Can I go now?' I asked.

'May I go now?' corrected Mr Papadopoulos.

'May I go now?' I repeated through gritted teeth.

Mr Papadopoulos hesitated and then he said, 'If you don't get at least a B on Friday's test, I'm going to have to get in touch with your uncle to suggest he hire a tutor.'

My stomach lurched even lower, which was funny as I thought it was already as low as it could go. Just shows, you can always sink further, I thought a little bitterly. Scott already had so much stuff going on with the court case and managing the clinic plus the CPZ job.

'I'll improve Mr Papadopoulos,' I said with a confidence I didn't feel.

'I hope so,' he said.

When I told Kylie about my conversation with *Paps*, she suggested we study math together all week after school in preparation for Friday's test. Kylie is much better at math than she thinks. If I even hear the word 'angle,' every brain cell I have seems to instantly shatter into dust.

Working our way through the problems at Kylie's apartment on Monday, we got stuck on some of them. We called Greg for help but he said, 'Hang on a minute, I'll see if Finn's here, he's a genius at math.'

'No,' I barked into the phone like a belligerent beagle. 'Um, Kylie and I want to try and figure it out ourselves. Thanks. Bye.'

Kylie looked at me curiously. There was a knock on her bedroom door. Kylie's mom, Rachel had arrived home from work. She insisted on cooking us a real, nutritional home-made meal, from scratch. Rachel's the worst cook on the face of the universe and every other part of the universe. Even toasting toast is a challenge for her. But Kylie and I did our best to choke down some of that ... well, whatever that burnt, sticky, rice dish was supposed to be.

'Yum, delicious,' said Kylie, which I think was taking the charade too far.

Worse was yet to come. After we stacked the dishes in the dishwasher, Rachel asked us to come with her to Camille's apartment. Camille's Mom, who is in the middle of a nasty divorce, had asked Rachel to appraise the value of the art-work in the apartment. Kylie and I made agonised faces at one another when Rachel's back was turned. Seeing Camille at school was bad enough. Having to go to her apartment and deal with her fake pity seemed too ... challenging. I wanted to say no, but I knew Kylie would never do that if she were me. Sometimes having friends with high moral standards can be a burden. They are a lot to live up to, I grumbled to myself as I followed Kylie and Rachel out into the rain.

It was dark and raining steadily by the time we reached Camille's apartment on East 85th Street. The housekeeper, Anya, let us in. She was not decked out like Eurdes in coloured satin bra, skirt with an elastic waistband and flip-flops. Anya wore a stiff old-fashioned black dress with a frilly white apron, like a maid in a PBS period costume drama. Anya led us through the long hallway into a strangely bare living room. Camille's Dad must have carted off half the furniture. I felt a little bad for Camille. It can't possible feel too good to watch your parents go three rounds over custody of an antique clock especially when neither of her parents seemed much interested in having custody of her.

Rachel wandered around the room scrutinising the paintings. Kylie and I sat down, squishing together on an uncomfortable but pretty cream-coloured chaise longue. We heard the clicking of heels in the hallway. The door opened and four people walked in.

'Hello, Evangeline,' said Leela in a friendly voice, as if the events of last summer had never happened.

My jaw dropped. I sat there, opening and closing my mouth like a goldfish with indigestion. Leela – enemy No. 1 from last summer! She was Scott's girlfriend at the time and basically made it her mission in life to marry him and turn him into a reality-TV show 'star' while shipping me home to Ireland, probably in a coffin if necessary. Thanks to Kylie and Greg and most especially Ben, I'd managed to … em … help her change her mind. Oh, and Scott woke up to the fact that his girlfriend was a Bride of Frankenstein type.

Camille's mom air kissed Rachel.

'Rachel, how lovely of you to drop by. This is Leela Patel, my divorce attorney, one of the best in the city, and, my daughter Camille, of course you know, and, this is my nephew Coltan.'

Coltan half-raised his eyebrows as a greeting. Rachel smiled all around and made polite small talk. I gripped the underside of the chaise longue.

'Your mouth's still open,' whispered Kylie pinching me on my arm.

I shut it. Coltan was looking at me, with a smarmy smile but without the furious hatred I thought I'd seen at Madison Square Garden. Still, it was too much, my three least favourite people all together in one room.

'I have to go home,' I said loudly. I'm not as good a person as Kylie is. I accept that.

'So soon,' said Leela. 'That's a pity. I didn't realise that Camille and Coltan were your friends.'

'She's not exactly our *friend*,' drawled Coltan.

I felt heat on my cheeks. It's not like I thought we were friends. I didn't even want to be his friend. But to hear him say it like that, in a tone that suggested friendship with me was equivalent to social suicide, embarrassed me.

Leela looked intrigued. She flashed Coltan one of her horribly-familiar seductive smiles. He looked bored. Leela, who was not used to that reaction from boys, sulked for a few seconds. Coltan watched her lazily as if he was the Queen Bee of the hive and she was one of his worker bees.

'You're a divorce lawyer,' he said to her. 'I'm interested in going to law school one day. Perhaps you would give me some tips on what courses I should study.'

Kylie and I stared at Coltan. He'd never remotely expressed any interest in studying law before or studying anything. But Leela looked gratified. She agreed at once. Then she turned her attention to Camille. I couldn't watch any more.

'Tell your Uncle Scott I said hi,' purred Leela as I stalked towards the door. There was something about the way she looked at me that was seriously unnerving; it was a *knowing* look but knowing what? I didn't stay around to try and find out. I left the room with as much dignity as I could muster, quelling with difficulty the instinct to run.

Kylie followed me to out to the hallway.

'So weird, she said, 'Leela, Camille and Coltan all together. It's like a convention of witches.'

'Yeah, real weird,' I agreed, 'Sorry to dump you with them but I can't hack making small talk with Leela. What am I supposed to do? Compliment her on her shoes?'

Kylie giggled and hugged me.

'I know, I know, it's OK, I can deal. Go home! See you tomorrow, text you later.'

I caught the M86 crosstown bus. I like the bus. It's slow, but that helps me think, and unlike the subway, there's stuff outside to look at. Bus passengers have a different energy to riders on the subway. Mostly, they are very, very old or kids, like me. Or they are in wheelchairs. On route, we picked up three different passengers in wheelchairs at three different

157

stops. At that last stop, the old lady in front of me with dyed plum hair and a scaly neck, started complaining very loudly about the delay caused when a passenger in a wheelchair got on the bus. Nasty old woman. I mean, seriously, surely, the passenger in the wheelchair has a LOT MORE to complain about. There was a young man in a Dunkin' Donuts uniform sitting beside her. When she started whining, he glared at her and stood up. There were no other free seats so he just stood there in the aisle with his back to her. I'm not sure, but I think she got the message because she stopped complaining.

Back home, I tried again to study for Friday's math test. By tried to study, I mean I spent an inordinate amount of time arranging my highlighters and shuffling things around. Meeting Leela had spooked me. I stared at the numbers in my book without seeing them. I saw only Leela's self-satisfied knowing smile, and Coltan's parting smirk. I couldn't concentrate on studying at all. I kept thinking about the court case. Somewhere along the way, it had assumed a whole life of its own; it was like an invisible fire-breathing, poisonous mythical creature that had taken up residence uninvited in our home and never had the manners to take even a single day off. The more I didn't study, the more panicked I became about Friday's math test.

\* \* \*

*Que sorpresa!* I blew it. The math test. I only got eight out of thirty questions right, and even getting those had been luck. It was a multi-choice test. If you pick enough 'c's' you're bound to get some right. Mr Papadopoulos didn't say anything to me when he handed me back my test paper. I avoided eye contact and held on to the faint hope that he'd forgotten his threat. When I got home after school, I made myself a peanut butter and banana sandwich and went down to the clinic still munching. I popped my head in the door of the examining room. Scott was treating a Dalmatian with a case of the hiccups, which didn't seem too serious but Malik, the Dalmatian's owner pointed out they'd lasted for more than a week. Scott looked pretty flummoxed.

'Hi, Scott,' I said, 'I'm going over to Greg's, I'll be back by six.'

'Not so fast, Evie,' he said. 'I need to talk to you about a call I had today from your math teacher. I'll be finished in the clinic in an hour or so. Go get on with your homework upstairs.'

Crapola. I dragged my feet up the spiral staircase, feeling a strong surge of resentment towards Mr Papadopoulos. Why couldn't he focus on his own life and stop sticking his big conk into mine?

Lost in my own thoughts as I wandered into the living room, it took me a few seconds to notice the couple passionately embracing on the couch. Horribly embarrassed, I was about to mumble, 'excuse me,' and back out of the room, when I remembered, hey I live here. I cleared my throat nosily. The couple sprang apart.

'Holly!' I said.

She giggled nervously and straightened her bra strap.

'Sorry if we gave you a scare Evie, this is Karl.'

'Hi,' said Karl.

'Hi,' I said back a little uncertainly. Holly was so pretty. What was she doing with such a gross-looking guy? He had a mullet haircut, which I'd never seen before except on TV and a tooth missing right near the front.

Karl stood up and gave Ben a pat and some treats out of his pocket.

'I gotta run,' said Karl, and he flicked me and Holly a sort of half-salute before sauntering out the door as if this was a hotel.

'KARL!' I said to Holly, 'OMG, isn't that your old boyfriend, the drug dealer, who threatened your old boss with a knife when he got out of jail?'

Holly's face turned faintly pink.

'He's changed! He's going straight now. He's turned his life around,' she said defensively.

I was just about to say something highly derogatory when I remembered Finn's reaction when I said druggies don't change. I felt ashamed of myself.

'Evie, please don't tell Scott, he might get mad and fire me,' begged Holly.

I hesitated. 'Holly, Scott wouldn't want that guy around here.'

Holly crossed the room and stood in front of me.

'Karl's drug days were a long time ago. He's changed. He's moved to New York to be with me. He's got a job at the gas station over on Tenth and he's training to be a mechanic. He deserves a second chance.'

I hesitated again.

'I won't have him around here again, I swear,' Holly said.

I remembered how nice Karl had been to Ben. Someone who likes animals can't be all bad.

'Ok,' I said, 'I won't say anything to Scott.'

'Thanks, Evie,' Holly said giving me a big hug. She smelt faintly of gasoline.

She left soon after that to go to her new restaurant job. For once, I was glad to see her go. I didn't have a good feeling. I didn't like keeping secrets from Scott. I already had the Lorcan and me secret and now I had another one. *Scott's Mr Laid-Back,* Joanna said once. (She didn't mean it as a compliment). Scott wouldn't be laid back about having Karl around. No way. But maybe Karl really had changed. I mean it was difficult but not impossible. Who Holly wanted to go out was Holly's business, I thought. I don't want to be some interfering busybody like Mr Papadopoulos!

Later that evening, Scott told me that he'd hired a math tutor to come by once a week to help me. Of all the tutors in all the schools in all the world, he chose Finn. Yep – Finn Winters, the guy who thinks of me as an almost kid sister. Great. Now I would be his *stupid*, almost kid sister. It was UNBEARABLE.

'Noooooo,' I begged.

Scott looked surprised. 'I thought you liked Finn.'

'I don't want him to be my tutor,' I said, 'he's only two

161

years older than me. If I have to have a tutor, shouldn't it be a real one. Or why can't you tutor me?'

'Me? I still count on my fingers and if I even hear the word "pie" and it doesn't involve eating, I feel frightened,' said Scott. 'And, I trust Finn,' he added decisively, 'this one isn't open for discussion. This isn't a democracy.'

'It's a dictatorship,' I moaned.

Scott looked unsympathetic. 'It's not forever, Evie, pull up your scores and if you do well in the rest of your tests then you won't have to go to summer school.'

'I'll go to summer school. Cancel Finn!'

'What's got into you, Evie?' said Scott, 'was there something strange in the peanut butter? Of course, you don't want to be in summer school when Kylie and Greg and loudmouth Lorcan and all your other friends are at the beach. Look, do a few sessions with Finn and let's see how it goes. If you don't feel he is helping, we'll find another tutor. Ok?'

'Ok,' I said, 'sorry about the money.'

'Stop worrying about the money. I got this covered. Give Finn a chance. Think about how it's going to look to the Judge if you are failing math under my care.'

I bit my lip and hung my head.

'I totally promise I'm going to try my best,' I said.

Scott grinned. 'Good attitude,' he said.

# Chapter 25

The humiliation of being tutored by Finn wasn't the only thing I worried about. Yesterday I felt pretty alarmed when Kylie, flung herself on my bed and pulled up the duvet so only her pink highlighted hair was visible. This wasn't the way she normally acted.

'Is everything ok?' I asked.

There wasn't any reply but some strange muffled noises.

'Are you *crying*?' I asked incredulously.

More muffled noises. I sat down beside her on the bed and rubbed her back because that's what my mum did to me when I cried when I was little and I didn't know what else to do. Kylie isn't a crier. Her mom, Rachel, once told me that Kylie hadn't even cried when she fell while she was performing on the ice two years ago and broke her left arm in two places.

Suddenly, a seed, a dark horrible thought formed in my mind and began to germinate. I said it quickly, the only way I knew how.

'It's not your Mom, is it? It's not Rachel. Is she … sick?'

Kylie sat up in the bed and faced me.

'Oh no, it's nothing like that.'

'Good,' I said relieved, 'well, how bad can it be? What's wrong? Please tell me. Maybe, I can help.'

And then it all came out so quickly and with so much sniffling that it was hard to follow but basically, she and Akono had broken up.

'Forever and ever,' Kylie added dramatically, 'he's so mean! I never want to see him again.'

While I think 'mean' is the very last adjective someone would use to describe Akono, this wasn't the time for semantics.

I nodded vigorously and offered Kylie some tissues.

I still wasn't clear on precisely what horrendous transgression Akono had committed. It seemed to start with him saying that she looked like a pink frosted cupcake and ending with him saying that she was full of *it*.

'Can you BELIEVE him?' Kylie asked, thumping my pillow vigorously.

'Yes,' I said.

'What?'

'I mean,' I said hurriedly, 'I believe Akono said that stuff but of course you are not full of *it*, whatever *it* is. And your hair doesn't remotely resemble a cupcake. The pink cupcakes have a much darker frosting.'

'I can't be with someone who doesn't fully support my dreams,' sniffed Kylie.

'No, of course not, you deserve so much better,' I answered.

Kylie smiled through her tears.

'Akono's not even cute!' she said.

'Not one bit cute,' I responded.

'And he thinks he's so smart and knows everything,' she added.

'Yeah,' I said, 'how smug! Annoying! Loser!'

'And those baggy jeans he insists on wearing make me want to barf,' Kylie added.

'I've never seen anyone with less fashion sense,' I said, 'those jeans do my head in. Do you want a slice of red velvet cake? I asked. 'Scott did an amazing job in saving a beagle puppy that had a horrible accident. It fell into the garbage disposal. His owner was so grateful, she baked the cake especially for Scott. It's the most fabulous cake ever!'

'I couldn't even swallow a tic-tac,' said Kylie, 'I'm way too distraught. Breaking up is so traumatic.'

'Exhausting!' I agreed although I didn't have any personal breaking-up experience. I hugged Kylie hard. I hated seeing her so upset.

I tried playing an upbeat boys band song to cheer her up.

'OMG! That was our song!' said Kylie.

I quickly switched it off.

'Ben!' I yelled and a minute later, Ben trotted in the room, yawning, one of his floppy ears, askew.

Kylie smiled. 'I love when his ear does that thing where it hangs over his head.'

I nodded. 'So cute!'

'Here, Ben,' I said, patting the space on the bed beside Kylie.

He jumped up and stretched out beside her. She scratched

his ears.

A few minutes later, she said solemnly, 'Akono is DEAD to me. D-E-A-D!'

'Dead to us!' I said.

'Thanks, Evie,' she sniffed, 'maybe I could manage a teeny slice of the red velvet cake, just a taster portion.'

'Of course,' I said delighted, 'good idea, I'll get it right away.'

# Chapter 26

A few minutes after five yesterday, we got the call every veterinarian dreads – Mrs Rubenstein. Every veterinary practice has its own Mrs Rubenstein. This time, she was calling about her favourite cat, Muffles. When Scott asked her to bring Muffles into the clinic, Mrs Rubenstein said in an offended tone,

'But it's raining. Cats don't like to get wet.'

'Nor do I,' replied Scott.

Joanna glared at him.

'Ok, ok, Mrs Rubenstein, one of us will be right over. What exactly is the problem with Muffles?'

'If I knew what the problem was, why would I be calling you?' Mrs Rubenstein said snottily.

Scott put his fist in his mouth and bit down on it before continuing.

'What are her symptoms?'

'She is distressed,' said Mrs Rubenstein.

'In what way is she distressed?' asked Scott.

'Severely! Is there any other way?'

Scott gave up at that point. He hung up and flipped a coin with Joanna to see which of them had to go. Joanna lost. (She shouldn't have let Scott do the toss. While I can't figure out how he did it, I strongly suspect he cheated. He must learn something from all those hours he spends watching poker on TV). I made the huge gesture of offering to accompany Joanna.

After helping her pack up all the stuff she thought we might need, we donned raincoats and headed out. As we splashed our way down Columbus Avenue, Joanna remarked that she hadn't seen much of Kylie around the place this week. (Joanna is *so* observant.)

'No, she's busy, school and stuff,' I said.

Joanna must have picked something up from the tone in my voice because she asked gently:

'Have you guys had a fight?'

'No, nothing like that. We never fight.'

'Ok,' said Joanna, and we crossed over and passed by the Lincoln Centre from which wafted the strains of an orchestra tuning up. We stopped in the rain to listen for a few moments.

'And ice-skating,' I said.

'What?' asked Joanna.

'Kylie. She's ramping up her ice-skating practice this year so that's why she's extra busy.'

'I see,' said Joanna, 'but the two of you are all good?'

'Oh, yeah,' I said, 'all good, well, except things are a bit awkward right now.' I continued in a rush. 'And, I don't know how to fix it,' I wailed. 'You see she and Akono broke up. She was really mad with him and upset and I kind of trashed Akono along with her. That's what good friends are supposed to do, right? Anyway, I agreed that he wasn't that cute, that kind of thing. I wanted to be on her side. Then a few days ago, out of nowhere, Kylie and Akono got back together. Now, Kylie keeps saying things like, "So you don't think Akono is that cute? And, you think he's smug?" and I don't, I really don't. I don't know what to say.'

Joanna stopped by the traffic lights and looked at me sympathetically.

'Evie, you've learned a valuable lesson the hard way. Never ever trash an ex unless you know the breakup is permanent and even then, don't do it.'

'I realise that now,' I said sadly as we reached Mrs Rubenstein's building.

The doorman on duty in her building was a woman with a long ponytail. I'd never seen a female doorman (or I suppose I should say doorperson) before. She seemed very put out that we were interrupting her phone conversation. She pointed at the elevator bank with a jerk of her thumb without pausing in her conversation.

We rode the elevator to the fourteenth floor. It's really the thirteenth floor but like a lot of buildings in Manhattan, they call it the fourteenth floor because it's difficult to rent apartments on the thirteenth floor. I'm not superstitious about the number thirteen. When I was in second class, I won a raffle by picking the number thirteen. The prize was rubbish, a book of Irish fairytales that I'd already read but still, thirteen is a lucky number for me.

To our surprise, Mrs Rubenstein's current husband, wearing an oversized woolen cardigan and the kind of slippers people steal from hotels, opened the door. We'd never met him before. Scott says Mrs Rubenstein doesn't allow him to leave the closet in their apartment.

Joanna said, 'Hi Mr Rubenstein, I'm Dr Barratt and this is Evie.'

I held out my hand, but Mr Rubenstein shrank away like he was frightened of my touch. Mrs Rubenstein appeared and barked at her husband,

'Harold, what are you doing out?' (Aha, so maybe Scott's theory had some substance after all, I thought).

The poor man looked scared. He shuffled off in his slippers.

Mrs Rubenstein turned her attention back to us.

'Muffles is this way,' she announced leading us through to the living room. The whole room was basically taken over by her three cats and all of their paraphernalia.

Muffles lay on her side in a soft red basket beside the TV.

'What seems to be the problem?' asked Joanna bending over to look at Muffles.

'She is suffering from some deeply troubling psychological issues that have manifested themselves in the form of excessive weight.'

'Excuse me?' said Joanna.

'She's gotten fat,' said Mrs Rubenstein.

'You asked us to make a house call because your cat's put on a little weight?' said Joanna coolly.

'This isn't any ordinary cat,' said Mrs Rubenstein haughtily, 'you can trace Muffles' bloodlines back to the Mayflower.'

Joanna sighed and bent down to examine Muffles. As she did so, I looked around the room. The walls were covered with blown-up photographs of the cover of Mrs Rubenstein's book as well as photographs of her with many different cats. But most of the photographs featured Muffles.

Joanna stood up and asked for some hot water. After washing and disinfecting her hands, she carried out an internal examination, anxiously watched by Mrs Rubenstein. Joanna looked up.

'Muffles doesn't have a weight problem.'

'Impossible,' said Mrs Rubenstein loftily, 'I weigh her every day.'

'The reason Muffles doesn't have a weight problem,' said Joanna as if Mrs Rubenstein had not spoken, 'is because she's pregnant.'

'TOTALLY IMPOSSIBLE,' roared Mrs Rubenstein, 'why I don't let that cat out of my sight. Nine months ago, we were in Palm Beach and she never left our hotel suite. To think you would accuse her of fornicating with some local common street cat, my poor baby.'

'Fine,' said Joanna rising to her feet, 'although you might feel a bit differently when the first kitten pops out, which I estimate will be in about fifteen minutes. Goodnight, Mrs Rubenstein.'

Mrs Rubenstein clutched wildly at Joanna's white coat.

'What? How?'

'Cats are pregnant for about nine weeks, not nine months,' said Joanna.

'My poor baby. Poor Muff. Oh, I bet it was that hideous common orange tomcat that that insufferable alcoholic in 2L lets run wild all around the building. I'm going to sue him for the rest of his life. Putting Muffles through this kind of trauma. What kind of genes could that thing pass on? He should be exterminated.'

I wasn't sure if she was talking about the cat or his alcoholic owner. Maybe both.

I saw Joanna mentally counting to ten, something she's taken on with lately to deal with stress.

After a deep breath, she said, 'Mrs Rubenstein, Muffles is about to bring her first set of babies into the world and I think she'll need all the help and support she can get from you at this time.'

Mrs Rubenstein looked stricken.

'Muff,' she said weakly, and then visibly pulling herself together, she began screaming for her housekeeper, 'Moola, towels, bring lots of towels.'

'No,' said Joanna calmly, 'best to avoid towels because the new kittens could easily get their claws caught on them. Do you have any old newspapers or even a sheet?'

'Call Scott,' Joanna said to me, 'and tell him we're going to be here for a while. I think Muffles is going to have a very large family.'

An hour later and two kittens had already arrived. The third was stuck. Joanna, very gently pulled the kitten out with a forceps, timing her pulling to coincide with Muffle's contractions. It was my job when the kittens were born to wipe their tiny little mouths and noses clear of mucus so they could breathe more easily. Five hours later, the last kitten, number six arrived.

'The other kittens are all bright orange but this one is black and white; he doesn't look anything like Muffles,' I said.

'Umm,' said Joanna, busy clearing up the rather disgusting mess of cat childbirth, 'a cat can give birth to kittens from different fathers in the same litter.'

Mrs Rubenstein reached out a hand to steady herself on a side table. 'I'm having palpitations,' she said weakly.

'But that's probably not the case here,' Joanna said hurriedly.

# Chapter 27

Nothing good ever happens on a Tuesday. I dawdled on my way home from school that Tuesday. Lorcan walked part of the way with me and we stopped for a slice of pizza. I wasn't even hungry. I was alone when I reached the corner of our block on Columbus and West 77th. There were two police cars outside our building and a bunch of cops milling around. A small crowd had gathered to watch, mainly doormen from the buildings along our block, a couple of security guards from the Natural History Museum across the street, the Mexican bus boys who worked in the kitchen at Scaletta and some excited looking tourists snapping photographs. They were blocking the sidewalk and I threaded my way through them feeling a bit of a thrill. Ours is a pretty quiet block. Not a lot of exciting stuff happens. Deirdre and Cate, my friends back in Dublin were kind of disappointed. At last, I'd have something to report. 'Oh yeah,' I would say casually, 'we had the police at our building arresting someone. They had their guns out. There was nearly a shoot-out.'

I squished my way near the front of the crowd just in time to see two cops push a handcuffed man into one of their cars.

'SCOTT,' I yelled and frantically began to fight my way through crowd.

'LET ME THROUGH, LET ME THROUGH,' I screamed, pushing as hard as I could.

By the time, I wriggled through the rest of the crowd; the police car had taken off, heading west. I could see the back of Scott's head. A cab on my side of the street with its light on was heading in the same direction. I flagged it down, yanked open the door, and nearly fell onto the black rubbery seat.

'GO,' I said and the taxi took off.

We reached the corner of the block. I could see the police car a couple of cars ahead heading south on Columbus.

'Downtown!' I said and we went around the corner and headed south.

There was a glass security partition between the driver and me. I rapped on it.

'Follow that police car in front,' I directed.

The taxi came to a halt so quickly that I banged my mouth against the glass and bit my tongue.

'Why are you stopping?' I gritted through the pain, 'keep following. We're going to lose him.'

'Get out kid,' said the driver, 'I'm not getting messed up with following no po-lice.'

'Pleaaaaaaaaase,' I said.

'Get out now before I *call* the police,' said the driver.

I jumped out of the cab and tried to flag another taxi down but none of them stopped. The police car had disappeared. I rubbed my swelling bottom lip. With shaking hands,

I pulled out my cell phone and hit 'J'.

'Please answer,' I whispered to myself.

'Hi, Evie,' said Joanna.

'It's me,' I said, 'It's Scott. The police have taken him. I don't know where. I don't know why.'

'What?' said Joanna.

'The police, they've arrested Scott.'

'When?' asked Joanna.

'A few minutes ago. I don't know where they're taking him.'

'Evie, calm down, listen to me, I'm going to make a few calls. Where are you now?'

'74th and Columbus,' I said.

'Go to the clinic and stay there. I will call you as soon as I find out where Scott is and what's going on. Send whatever people are waiting to Peter's clinic and tell Holly to close down the clinic for the rest of the day.'

'Ok,' I said and she hung up.

# Chapter 28

I helped Holly close up the clinic. She couldn't tell me much except that the police had turned up with an arrest warrant for Scott. She had no idea why. Kylie called but I let it ring through to voicemail because I didn't want to risk missing Joanna's call. She did some pretty fast work because in about half an hour, she called. Scott was being held at the police precinct on West 35th Street between 8th and 9th. Joanna was there now. She had been in touch with Scott's lawyer, Rob, who had jumped in a cab and was on his way to the station.

'How is Scott doing?'

'They won't let me see him yet,' said Joanna.

'But why was he arrested?' I asked.

'It doesn't make sense,' said Joanna, 'something to do with supplying illegal drugs. Apparently, the detectives traced painkillers and sedatives back to our clinic. It has to be some huge mistake. The drugs cabinet hasn't been broken into and the only people who have keys are Scott and me. We don't even let Karen or Holly have a key.'

'I'll meet you at the station. I'll be there in ten minutes,' I said.

'No,' said Joanna, 'it's no place for you. Stay at home and I'll call as soon as I have more news.'

'No, I want to go.'

'I know you do, sweetheart,' said Joanna, 'but Scott wouldn't want you to be here.'

'But I have to be there,' I wailed.

'It will be harder on Scott if you're here,' said Joanna.

I felt like kicking something because I knew she was right. Scott would hate to have me in the police station. It can be so frustrating sometimes being a kid.

'Ok,' I said grudgingly, 'please call me as soon as you know anything. ANYTHING, even if it's something really small.'

'I promise,' said Joanna.

As soon as I'd hung up, I turned to Holly and told her about the drugs charge.

'Evie, I know what you're thinking but it couldn't have been Karl. He couldn't have stolen the drugs. I don't have a key to the cabinet.'

I felt a little guilty because as soon as Joanna had mentioned the word 'drugs,' I'd instantly thought of Karl but Holly was right. She didn't have a key.

I went up to the apartment. Holly insisted on coming along and keeping me company but I wasn't in the mood for talking. I went into my room to be alone, leaving her in the living room, watching TV. I wished Mum were here. I kind of half-wished Finn was here but I banished that thought.

I tried to keep my mind focused on the crime. There were only two keys to the drugs cabinet. Joanna always kept hers on her. So did Scott except sometimes, at night, he left it out on the kitchen table. Holly's never here at night and there's no way someone could have come into the apartment and stolen the key. Even if he or she had a key to the door and got past the doormen, they'd never get around Ben. He was an amazing watchdog. He'd bark the whole building awake if a stranger came into the apartment.

A person could go totally crazy thinking, I thought. I called Kylie but she was at ice-skating practice. I called Greg next and explained everything. He insisted on coming over straight away. It was only much later that I realised it had never occurred to me to call Lorcan.

Greg brought some burritos with him, but I couldn't eat. We sat cross-legged on the floor of my room, trying to figure out how someone could have stolen drugs from the clinic. Greg asked me to think back on any suspicious characters hanging around the clinic but I couldn't think of any. We had some highly eccentric people coming in and out all the time but criminals, no. I kept coming back to Karl and finding him in the apartment that time.

'Tell me again what happened. Leave nothing out,' said Greg.

'I've already gone through this with you twice. Nothing. I came in. Holly and Karl were kissing. They got up. Karl said 'hi'. He did this kind of half-salute thing and he left. There was nothing more to it.'

'Are you sure,' said Greg, 'think again.'

I frowned at him but I obediently closed my eyes. I could

see Karl's mullet and the space near the front of his mouth where a tooth was missing. I could smell the faint trace of gasoline from his clothes and from Holly's.

'OH MY GOD,' I said opening my eyes, and hitting Greg on the shoulder much harder than I intended.

'Owww,' he said, rubbing his arm, 'take it easy, what is it?'

'Ben! Ben was there. In the apartment. Karl was being really nice to him. He even gave him some treats.'

'So. Karl likes dogs. So what?' said Greg.

'Karl could have used Holly's key to get into the apartment. He could have easily slipped it out of her purse, even had a copy made. If he came in here, Ben wouldn't bark because he wouldn't think of Karl as a STRANGER. And God knows how many times Karl was here before I caught them. So Ben was used to him being around.'

'Come on,' I said to Greg.

I dashed out into the living room.

'Holly,' I said, 'Is Karl a dog person?'

'What do you mean?' she asked looking bewildered.

'Is Karl into dogs?'

'No, he doesn't like dogs or cats or any animals or … children or old people. They're not his thing.'

I turned triumphantly to Greg. 'We're gonna get that guy!'

\* \* \*

The hardest part was convincing Holly to go with us to the police station. At first, she kept insisting that Karl was innocent. After a little while, she said, she didn't know anymore.

'You DO know,' I said forcefully, 'deep down somewhere inside, you know that Karl did this. You have to come with us and tell the police about him and where he lives.'

Holly got this stubborn look in her eyes and I felt a rush of anger with her.

'Oh my God, Holly, think of everything Scott has done for you! He gave you a job and a place to hang out and he paid you your salary in advance lots of times when you were broke. Are you really going to let him rot in jail for years to save a loser like Karl?'

'People don't rot in prison anymore,' said Greg, 'they have all kinds of stuff like creative writing programs and cooking classes.'

I glared at Greg.

'Sorry,' he mumbled, 'I was just saying—'

'I'll do it,' said Holly, 'I'll tell the police about Karl and where he lives. Maybe they will find that he had nothing to do with this.'

Well, that didn't happen because when the police searched Karl's apartment, they found drugs from our clinic in his bathroom.

But that happened later, after the police had released a very subdued Scott. He'd only been under arrest for about six hours but it felt like days. His homecoming wasn't as joyous as I thought it was going to be. He looked tired. So did Joanna. They both stood around awkwardly in the living room as if they'd never been here before. Scott reached out and touched Joanna's face.

'What is that?' he said holding up a finger covered with some kind of green mushy cement.

'Oh,' said Joanna looking embarrassed, 'I was having a facial in Ling down by Union Square when I got Evie's call. I splashed some water on my face, but I guess I must have missed some spots.'

'Joanna,' said Scott, 'I don't know how to thank you. I—'

'No need to thank me. No big deal,' said Joanna hurriedly. 'Get some sleep, I'm helping you with Missy's operation first thing in the morning, remember.'

After Joanna left, Scott had the longest shower of his life. Afterwards, he said he still stank like a police cell. Smelly or not, I was relieved to have him home. If I had told Scott about finding Karl in the apartment that time, none of this would have happened. I tried to apologise to Scott but he wasn't mad with me. He said he was equally to blame for being so cavalier about hiring Holly and giving her a key to our home. I don't think either of us felt very good about ourselves.

I felt even worse the next day when I turned up at school to find out that Camille had posted on her blog that my uncle had been arrested for drug dealing. I blamed Greg. He had gone straight to his Young Film-Makers of Tomorrow class the night before and used Scott's arrest as a plot for his screenplay. Writers have no shame. His screen-writing buddy, Luca, had told someone who told someone who told someone until eventually it ended up on Camille's blog. I felt all agitated and panicky. I couldn't sit still and conjugate Spanish verbs. I thought about what I should do. I could go to the school principal and report Camille. I was pretty sure the principal would make her take down the post and she'd get into a lot of trouble. But so far, the kids at school hadn't shown much interest in checking out Camille's page. If the principal made her take it down then EVERYONE would want to know about it. Sometimes, I thought, it's better to do nothing. I'm not scared of Camille. She's just a kid. But I might be a little scared of Leela. She is an adult. She has power.

# Chapter 29

It's bizarre how one week your life is so overflowing with people and pets that you barely have time to live it and the next, they are gone and you don't know how to fill the spaces they have left behind.

Three days after Scott's prison break (well, that's what we called it), when he and I returned to the clinic after a trip to visit a penguin at the CPZ, we found Holly in the waiting room surrounded by two suitcases and two black garbage bags overflowing with her possessions. Buddy lay beside her on the floor snoring. He'd picked up Ben's enviable knack for having a snooze anytime anywhere.

Scott and I stared at the packed suitcases in surprise.

'What's going on here? You're leaving?' asked Scott.

Holly's face turned a little pink.

'The teacher of my improvisation class thinks I've got great comic timing and he's arranged an audition for me with an improv group in Chicago. He thinks I have a real shot at it.'

'Of course you do. You'll be terrific,' said Scott.

'But why can't you do improv here! Who would want to leave New York?' I wailed.

'You did. Last summer. You wanted to go back to Ireland,'

said Scott.

Scott always has a perfect memory at the most inconvenient times.

'Yes, well, I do love Ireland equally, but we're talking about HOLLY now, not me.'

Scott turned back to Holly.

'Holly, we've talked about this. Of course, I was furious with you for having Karl anywhere near Evie and our home. But I appreciate the courage it took for you to turn him in. You've become part of our family here at the clinic. Stay with us!' he said and he gave that little smile that all women (except for Joanna and Mrs Rubenstein, oh and his bookkeeper Virpi), seem to find so irresistible.

Holly smiled back. 'Thank you,' she said, 'but I'm not part of the *us*. Not really. I don't belong in a veterinary practice. I don't belong here the way Joanna does. I need to go find my life.'

Scott went to say something but Holly put her finger to his lips and kissed him softly on the cheek. Then she hugged me. I got down on my knees and gave Buddy a big hug.

'Gonna miss you,' I said, 'both of you.'

And I do. I miss them both … Ben only misses Holly.

So, boom! Just like that. Holly and Buddy were gone. The next boom sounded two days later while I was stretched out on the couch playing a game battling a team of evil, giant-sized hares who try to take over LA. Eurdes was in the kitchen and I overheard her say,

'Dr Brooks, I need serious talk with you.'

My fingers stilled on the control pad and I lifted my head to listen. I didn't like the sound of this.

'What is it Eurdes?' asked Scott.

'I can't take it no more,' wailed Eurdes, 'it's not natural. In my country, we do not live like this with those dirty things in our houses, only clean ones, like chickens and we eat them.'

'Excuse me?' said Scott.

'I am always work, work, work and it's not easy but I never complains,' said Eurdes in a complaining tone, 'and you, Dr Brooks, you are a good employer, my best employer. I can't thank you enough for the ticket home to Brazil for Christmas. Such generous of you and you have no moneys. Of all the people I work for you, you have the most littlest moneys.'

'Good to know,' said Scott dryly.

'Mrs Bradford, you know what she geeves me for the holidays?'

And before allowing Scott time to respond, Eurdes continued, 'I work for her and her cheeldrins and her husband three days a week for fifteen years now. At Christmas, does she give me moneys? No, she gives me a present all wrapped up in a box. I say, thank you and I think maybe it will be ok. Do you know what she geeves me?'

'I'm going go out on a limb here and guess it wasn't something overly thoughtful,' said Scott.

'A miniature golf set for playing on the carpet!' announced Eurdes. 'I didn't even know what that was. Do I looks like to you I would play golf on my floor?'

'No,' agreed Scott.

'So Dr Brooks, I love working for you and I don't want to leeves you and Evie but I can't take the dirty bird pooping all the time.'

'Ah,' said Scott, 'you mean Evie's pigeon, Persie.'

'Si, si, Pigeon.'

'EVIE,' called Scott.

For a microsecond, I considered a quick dash out the front door but thought what's the point; I might as well get it over with. I strolled into the kitchen area.

'Greg gave Persie to me as a birthday present,' I explained to Scott, 'not a very thoughtful one so I can totally appreciate Eurdes's feelings on the miniature golf set. What a useless present! What's the worst present you have ever received Scott?'

Scott wasn't interested in being drawn into a diverting conversation about horrendous presents.

'Evie, I'm sorry. Persie has to go. Today!'

'Thank you Dr Brooks,' purred Eurdes.

'But Scott, Persie has been domesticated. I don't think he'd survive out in the real world anymore,' I protested.

Scott handed me his iPad. 'So get busy on locating a new home for him,' he said mercilessly, 'and you owe Eurdes an apology!'

'Sorry, Eurdes,' I said.

'That's ok,' she said magnanimously.

I very quickly managed to find a fantastic home for Persie, with Juan, one of our doorman, who had always admired him and seemed thrilled to take him off my hands. Greg said that Juan likes to eat pigeon, but that was a joke in very poor taste.

So boom, just like that, Persie was gone. The third boom happened while Lorcan and I were eating burgers at the Shake Shack at the end of my block. Lorcan casually announced that he would be leaving New York to go live in Hong Kong for at least a month, maybe longer. I choked on a fry. A beefy man in a grey hoodie at the next table leapt off his stool, threw his arms around my chest and began heaving me up and down in some kind of misguided effort to perform the Heimlich manoeuvre. I don't want to sound ungrateful (even to myself) but the guy nearly killed me. One of his gold chains got entangled around my neck and I nearly choked to death. Plus, I was mortified. I challenge anyone to retain even a semblance of dignity when they are being bounced up and down like that and anyway; I had swallowed the fry before he even started so it was completely unnecessary. The man took a lot of convincing to be persuaded that I was perfectly alright (except for the red rope burn on my neck caused by his chain) and to put me down. I also forced myself to thank him even though I felt some kind of law should be passed prohibiting him from trying to rescue people.

When he had finally returned to his own table, Lorcan gave me the lowdown on the whole Hong Kong trip. Peter, one of Lorcan's dads, had to go back to Hong Kong to work on some software project. Lorcan's other dad, Simon, said that the family had to stick together and that there was no way that he was letting Peter off by himself in the nightclubs of Hong Kong to be hit on by the entire Asian gay community. Lorcan said that Simon was overrating Peter's level of attractiveness but I thought it was sweet.

'When are you leaving?' I asked.

'Tomorrow,' said Lorcan.

'Oh,' I said, 'are you ok with that?'

'Sure, a month off school, hanging around Hong Kong, that's fine with me, but I'll miss you.'

I looked at him surprised. Lorcan and I don't do the ordinary typical mushy boy-girl compliment thing. I wondered if he was being sarcastic, but he looked sincere.

'Oh,' I said.

'How about you'll miss me too?' Lorcan asked in a voice that was half-kidding, half not.

'Of course I'll miss you,' I said and he smiled.

It was true that I would miss him. I'd miss any of my friends who left. But I wasn't sad. I actually felt kind of relieved to be spared the whole angst of figuring out how I felt about Lorcan and what to tell Scott about us. Now, Lorcan would be away for a month, plenty of time for me to figure things out.

I went round to Lorcan's apartment early the next morning before school to say good-bye. It was a fairly dramatic parting and I quite enjoyed playing the role of grieving girlfriend as if I was sending him off to war in the Middle East. I threw a lot of energy into it. I might have overplayed the role a little, but Simon loved it.

We didn't kiss good-bye because Lorcan's dads were there. I felt sort of relieved by that. I haven't much felt like kissing Lorcan since the day of the ice hockey game. I don't know why. Maybe it was watching him eat that horrible orange cheese sauce on the nachos. Maybe I am that shallow. I shouldn't have played the part of the dutiful girlfriend. I might have misled Lorcan into thinking I'm more into him than I am. But I'm not sure how into him I am. Maybe, I'm more into him than I think. Life was less complicated before boys.

# Chapter 30

We had our pretrial conference today. This was the fourth time Scott and I had to go to court so we were pretty complacent this morning because nothing much ever seems to happen. Oh. Something unusual did occur the last time, though; Scott and I were horrified to see Leela and Mr Tully deep in conversation outside the courtroom. But when we told Rob that we were worried about what they might be up to, he assured us that we were just being paranoid; that the New York family law world is very small and everyone knows everyone and Mr Tully and Leela were probably working on another case together. Scott seemed reassured by this. And, as he reminded me, he still had the tape I had made last year which would get Leela in a whole heap of trouble if he put in the hands of the authorities or even the press.

'So you see,' he said, 'if anyone should be worried, it's Leela, not us.'

'I guess,' I said but I was still troubled by the knowing smile Leela had shot me in Camille's apartment. But seriously, how do you explain that without sounding crazy. I let it drop.

Early this morning, Scott and I stood in the security line at 60 Centre Street. We could easily pick out the people who were going to court for the first time. They looked nervous and intimidated and lost. Scott and I probably looked as bored as the rest of the regulars. We had no idea of the shock heading our way.

When the court clerk called our case, the judge didn't usher the lawyers into his room for some private chitchat and a few laughs like he usually did. This time we sat at two separate tables in front of the judge's desk, Michael and Mr Tully at the table on the right and Scott, Marcy and me, at the table on the left. Rob couldn't make it because his son, Harry, had chicken pox. He'd sent along a junior lawyer from his office instead, a young, pretty, fidgety woman named Jessica. She looked so pale and frightened that I felt sorry for her. When the clerk called our case, she was nowhere to be seen.

'Probably throwing up in the bathroom,' Marcy said.

Marcy was not her usual bubbly self. She was acting a little odd. She was very cold to Scott. She barely even said 'hello' to him. But she kept acting all protective towards me as if I was a child star who needed to be shielded from the paparazzi.

The judge got straight to the point. He said he had received the forensic reports except for the Neutral's because she was suffering from exhaustion and had to take a couple of weeks of vacation.

Scott and I exchanged worried glances. Nobody had told

us that the reports had been filed or that Rosita had gone away. The judge took his glasses off and began cleaning them vigorously with a dusty yellow scrap of cloth.

'I have to say that I am deeply disturbed by the contents of Dr Blakely's report, which presents a sordid tale of drugs and other questionable activities engaged in by Dr Brooks,' said the Judge. 'And Dr Brook's own psychologist, Mary-Ann, seems to think that he is not a fit guardian.'

Mr Tully jumped to his feet, waving around what appeared to be a copy of Dr Blakely's report. There were about fifty yellow post-it notes sticking out from it. So, everyone got the report but us, I thought sourly.

Mr Tully totally exaggerated the circumstances behind Scott's arrest and began raving that my safety and wellbeing were in serious jeopardy.

Scott leaned over me and whispered angrily to Marcy, 'I was never charged! He's totally misleading the judge. Object or something.'

'I represent Evie, not you,' said Marcy and she reached down and squeezed my hand.

'It's so unfair that Michael and his lawyer got the reports and we didn't,' I said to her.

'Oh, I got them. I didn't want to upset you with the details. I am very worried about you,' she said, her eyes all big and Bambi's-motherish. 'And MaryAnn strongly feels that Scott is not an appropriate guardian for you.'

I almost screamed. 'MaryAnn,' I said furiously, 'is just mad with Scott because he doesn't want to DATE HER.'

'Marcy,' hissed Scott leaning over me again, 'I'm sure the Blakely report reflects badly on me, but I can explain everything. Didn't Rob tell you what happened?'

'No smoke without fire,' Marcy whispered back cryptically and I felt like a cold ghostly finger had just trailed down my back.

Marcy got to her feet. Mr Tully eyed her warily.

'Your Honour,' said Marcy, 'on the basis of disturbing information that has come to light, I am substituting my judgment for my client's because I do not feel that, at this time, Evangeline is able to give instructions in accordance with her own best interests.'

'What are you talking about?' I asked, confused, tugging Marcy's sleeve.

She patted me lightly on the head.

'This is for your own good, Evie,' she whispered, 'let me do my job, I'm taking care of it.'

'What?' I said but Marcy continued with her speech to the judge.

'And so, your Honour, in light of the respondent's recent arrest, I am advocating that custody be temporarily transferred to the petitioner, Michael Carey, with supervised visitation for the uncle respondent. In due course, down the line, I hope we could move to a schedule of unsupervised visitation if the respondent agrees to regular screening for drug problems.'

My heart stopped beating for a few seconds. Greg told me later that that is medically impossible. Whatever. I know what I felt. My heart STOPPED! TRAITOR. TREACH-ERY. BETRAYED BY MY OWN LAWYER.

Without even thinking about it, I jumped to my feet, quickly followed by Scott.

'Your Honour,' we said in unison.

'SIT DOWN,' thundered the Judge, 'lawyers only!'

Scott reluctantly sat down, but I remained on my feet.

'But my lawyer is betraying me,' I said, 'my welfare isn't remotely in danger. Marcy doesn't know what she's talking about. Scott doesn't have any drug problems. He was just being nice to Holly and it was her ex-boyfriend Karl who stole the drugs and ...'

'Miss Brooks,' interrupted the Judge, 'you are represented by a lawyer who speaks on your behalf. You are not permitted to address the court directly. Your lawyer will explain this to you after the conference if she has not already done so.'

'Fine,' I said, 'she's fired. I must have the right to fire my own lawyer! I want to represent myself. Now may I address you?'

'Your Honour,' said Marcy, rolling her eyes and smiling in a conspiratorial way at the Judge, 'my client is going through the very traumatic process of a custody case. She's having trouble processing it all. She doesn't know her own mind. I'll speak to her as soon as we're done here.'

'Your former client doesn't seem traumatised to me at all,' boomed the Judge, 'she seems like a young lady very much in tune with her own mind. I want to hear what she has to say,' and turning to his clerk, he said, 'what date do I have available next week? I want to set up a Lincoln interview.'

There was silence in the courtroom as the clerk thumbed the pages of the judge's calendar. Scott took my hand.

'Wednesday looks good, judge,' said the clerk.

'What about late afternoon, say four-thirty?' said the judge, 'I don't want Miss Brooks to miss any more school.'

'Four-thirty works,' said the clerk.

'Good,' said the judge.

'Miss Brooks, a Lincoln interview is just the legal name for a meeting between you and me with no lawyers present. Ok?

'Ok,' I said, still standing.

'It's nothing for you to get nervous about. It's just an opportunity for you and me to talk so I can listen to what you have to say.'

'Thank you, Your Highness,' I said fervently, 'sorry, I mean, Your Honour.'

He nodded at me.

Mr Tully rose to his feet.

'Judge, I really don't think this is a case where a Lincoln interview is necessary or appropriate. In the *Parkinson* case, the Court of Appeals clearly held that where ...'

'Mr Tully,' interrupted the judge, 'you're surely not proposing to lecture me on the *Parkinson* case. I think we can all take it as a given that I am familiar with the Court of Appeal's ruling in that case. I have ordered a Lincoln interview. If you disagree with that, you are familiar with the appeal process and you have sufficient time between now and Wednesday to make whatever motion you are going to make.'

'Yes, Judge,' said Mr Tully, 'may I request a stay?'

'You may so request and that request is denied,' said the judge.

'Judge,' said Marcy, 'I can't be here on Wednesday afternoon. I have a case in Westchester.'

'Since you are no longer representing any party in this case, your presence will not be required,' said the judge.

'But Judge, you're surely not going to permit my thirteen-year-old client to fire me.'

'I already have,' said the judge smoothly. He continued, 'Now, we've already overrun and I have fifteen more cases on my calendar today.'

The judge stood up, resplendent in his black robes and swept out of the room as if he was a much taller man.

'Evie, let me explain, we can work this out, I'm looking after your best interests,' said Marcy.

'I don't want anything to do with you ever again,' I said quietly, and, Scott and I left the courtroom.

I mean really. I knew Marcy thought she was doing the right thing. But she had no right to jump to the conclusion that Scott was mixed up in drugs.

* * *

That night, I had one of my tutoring sessions with Finn. He takes being a tutor so seriously, it's annoying. He never talks about anything but math. But this time, he said,

'I hear from Greg that Lorcan's gone to Singapore.'

'Hong Kong,' I corrected.

'Right,' he said and he seemed very pleased, no doubt because he thinks I'm too much of a baby to have a boyfriend.

'How's the custody case going?' he asked.

'Fine,' I lied in a chirpy tone, glancing at the thin white scars on his arms.

He scowled at me and pulled his shirtsleeve down.

'What's your lawyer like?' he asked after a few seconds.

'I don't have one. I fired her,' I snapped.

'What? You fired her?' and he laughed.

I glared at him.

'Could we please move on to problem seventeen because I've got stuff to do later, stuff that has nothing to do with math.'

'Sure,' he said, still grinning.

'Great,' I said.

'Great,' he said.

'Great,' I repeated. (Dumb I know).

I'm not interested in discussing my private business with someone who thinks I'm a little kid. And I'm fed up with Finn acting like a big brother trying to sort out my problems. He's not my brother! He should be spending his time working on his own multiple issues.

# Chapter 31

Looking back now, it feels like the trial happened to someone else, someone who looked like me, but was not me. It began on the same day Mum died exactly one year ago. I thought that might mean something, but maybe it just worked out that way in order to accommodate the Judge's dental appointments. He scheduled the trial to last a full eleven and one-half days spread over the month of May.

And so it began. Monotonous. Boring. Slow. Did I say TEDIOUS? On the plus side, I wasn't nervous. I'll say this for boredom – it kills anxiety. Also, I'd been to the Lincoln interview with the Judge and I think that went pretty well. He was much nicer when he was in his office without his formal black gown, more approachable, almost human. He gave me some stale goldfish crackers and talked about his granddaughter who lives in California. I told him Scott was the best guardian anyone could hope for and he seemed to believe me.

The trial days began to blend into one another. I quickly adjusted to our new routine. Get up. Walk Ben. Eat Breakfast. Go To Court. Come Home. Eat Chinese/Thai/Indonesian/

Turkish/Greek Food with Scott and Rob. Discuss the day's testimony. Repeat.

Joanna ate with us some nights, which was great, like old times, except sometimes we had to put up with her boyfriend, Jeffrey, too. Scott says he makes Joanna's old boyfriend, Stefan, seem charismatic. Joanna's covering all the work at the clinic so Scott can fully concentrate on the trial and get this, she never ever complains about it or tries to make him feel bad. Scott said that's super annoying.

As the petitioner, Michael got to put forward his side of the case first. Dr Blakely, as repulsively tanned and God-like as ever, was the first witness. He described Scott as irresponsible and immature, the kind of person who permits a drug-dealer and a convicted felon to have free access to his apartment.

I fared little better. According to Dr Blakely, I suffered from a lack of moral guidance and stable adult supervision. He also described me as having violent tendencies apparently on the basis of an incident at my former school in Ireland where I threw a pencil case at a boy in my class.

The second witness was Holly's former boss, the guy from the Peruvian restaurant, only too eager to talk about Karl's knife attack on him. I think it was the only exciting thing that ever happened to him in his life. It was all so stupid. . . Scott has never even *met* Karl!

Next came the endless talk about the supposedly irresponsible state of Scott's finances. It was so boring that I dozed off a lot. So did Scott. Finally, the Judge got almost as fed up as we were and said very sarcastically to Mr Tully, that he should bring the financial evidence to a quick conclusion because Scott's veterinary practice was not a party seeking custody of the young lady in this case. (I HATE being called young lady. It's so patronising).

Mr Tully, said, 'Certainly, your Honour. I believe we have more than sufficiently shown that the petitioner, a successful music producer in Australia is in a much better position to provide this child with a secure, stable and privileged life-style.'

Next came evidence about my math test scores, but only the ones from the middle of the year, the ones that I had failed miserably. Mr Tully, didn't, of course, mention the more recent tests, which, thanks to Finn's help, I had pretty much aced. Rob kept reminding Scott and me that we would get our chance to cross-examine and also to put forward our own witnesses. I guess that kept us going. And anyway, the Judge couldn't care less about my poor math scores. He said,

'If math test scores were an appropriate barometer of parental fitness; most of the parents in America would lose their children.'

We were almost giddy with relief heading in to court on the sixth day because finally it was our turn to tell our side. The trial was scheduled to continue at ten. A few minutes before ten, just as the Judge entered the courtroom, Mr Tully handed Rob copies of his 'Amended Witness List.' 'Two new witnesses,' he said.

'You've got to be kidding!' said Rob, 'you can't give us notice of new witnesses at this stage, it's far too late.'

There followed lots of arguing in front of the judge. He actually said, 'Approach the bench counselors,' just like on TV. We lost.

Mr Tully called the first new witness. The back doors of the courtroom creaked open and in walked ... Camille, looking absurdly angelic with her braided white-blonde hair, her navy dress with a wide white collar and patent black Mary Jane shoes. As she reached the top of the courtroom, I stood up and stepped out from the desk, blocking her path.

'CAMILLE, what are you doing here?'

She hesitated and looked at Mr Tully. He nodded encouragingly at her.

'Sit down Miss Brooks,' boomed the judge.

I sat down reluctantly on the very edge of my chair.

Mr Tully was all solicitous concern in his questioning. After saying her name and address, Camille looked downwards coyly at her feet as if too shy and overwhelmed to speak. The judge smiled at the pretty picture she made. I thought I was going to puke.

'Take your time, Camille,' said Mr Tully; 'I want you to tell the Court about the events of March fifteenth of this year.'

'Evie, umm, Evangeline and I were the only two girls left in the locker room at school. As we were changing, I noticed she had these strange bruises on her arms.'

'Exhibit 17 Your Honour,' said Mr Tully, handing around photographs of me with clearly bruised arms. It was me alright in the pictures. Camille must have taken them on her phone when I wasn't looking. So creepy.

'Camille, did your friend, Evie, say how she got those bruises?' Mr Tully asked.

'She's not my friend,' I said, standing up.

'It's true that hasn't been established,' said the judge, 'move on Mr Tully.'

Camille smiled a tiny smile at me before raising her squinty little eyes to the Judge.

'Evie told me that the night before, her Uncle Scott lost his temper and grabbed her by her arms and shook her because he was so mad that she had burnt something in the microwave.'

'What?' Scott and I both yelled, jumping to our feet.

'Judge, that's not true, it's a big fat grotesque lie. I got those bruises from trying to learn to skateboard,' I said.

The judge looked down at me.

'Off the record,' he said to the stenographer.

'Evie,' said the judge, 'Was anyone with you when you fell of your skateboard.'

'Just Ben,' I said.

'Who is Ben? Is he a classmate at school?'

'Your Honour,' said Mr Tully, 'Ben is the respondent's DOG.'

'I see,' said the judge, 'continue Mr Tully, I'll allow you a couple of more questions.'

Mr Tully turned to Camille.

'Can you remember anything else Evie said to you in the

changing room?'

Camille screwed her face up very tightly as if trying to remember each specific detail exactly.

'I think she said it was rice that she burnt in the microwave but I'm not one hundred percent sure,' she said.

'Could I have a glass of water,' she added.

The security guard gave her a little plastic cup.

She sipped the water with trembling hands. The judge looked sympathetic.

'Are you ready to continue?' asked Mr Tully.

'I'll do my best,' said Camille sweetly. 'I told Evie to tell one of our teachers or the school nurse about what her uncle Scott had done to her but she was too afraid.'

'How do you know she was afraid Camille?' asked Mr Tully in a pseudo gentle tone.

'Because she said that if anyone found out, her uncle Scott would make her pay.'

'YOU DISGUSTING SICK LIAR,' I yelled jumping to my feet again.

'Your Honour,' said Mr Tully, 'I think we can all appreciate how difficult it is for Evie to relive this. Perhaps it would be wise to excuse her from the proceedings.'

'No, No,' I said, clenching my fists 'I'm not reliving anything. It didn't happen. Scott never shook me. He's never hurt so much as a flea in his life.'

'Your Honour,' said Mr Tully, 'I have here police records from South Carolina detailing Dr Brooks past record of violence.'

'Are you for real?' said Scott, 'this is a farce! That was just a brawl at a college game more than a decade ago. Everyone was arrested.'

'Control your client,' the judge said to Rob and Rob tugged on Scott's sleeve.

'Mr Tully,' said the judge, 'you are treading in dangerous territory. Is this all you have? The evidence of a teenage schoolgirl and some obsolete police reports.'

'No, your Honour, I have another witness,' said Mr Tully.

'Call your next witness,' said the judge, 'and be quick about it. It's nearly lunchtime. You may excuse your witness but you will need to have her back in court next week for cross-examination assuming I don't throw this whole side-show out.'

Camille stepped down from the witness stand and began to walk towards the door. About halfway, she stopped, and turned and looking directly back at me, said,

I'm so sorry Evie to betray your confidence but sometimes we need to have the courage to help our friends even when they don't want it.'

I glared at her so stunned by her deviousness that I couldn't speak; the only sound that came out of my mouth was a small choking sound.

The next witness sauntered into the courtroom. Coltan! He said that I had told him that Scott frequently locks me into my bedroom at night when he is drinking. Unlike Camille, he never made eye contact with me. He spoke clearly and without emotion, looking only at the judge and Mr Tully.

He scared me. I wanted to jump up and fight but I was too dizzy to move. My legs had stopped working. It was like having the most excruciating case of pins and needles. I sat slumped in my chair, my mind whirring painfully. LEELA! I thought. She's the one behind this. She put them up to it. She's getting her revenge.

I tried to focus on what the judge was saying.

'It's getting late. We're going to adjourn until Monday morning. Some very serious allegations have been made and while I appreciate that the respondent has not yet had the opportunity to cross-examine or to answer those allegations, I'm going to err on the side of caution in the interests of the child's safety. I'm going to make a temporary order making the subject child of the proceedings a ward of the State of New York. Social services will take her into custody for the weekend and I'll see everyone back here on Monday morning. And, I'm going to make a stay-away as part of the order. Dr Brooks, you may not see or communicate with your niece until Monday morning. If you breach my order, the consequences will be very serious.'

Scott was whispering to Rob who got up.

'Your Honour, I respectfully request that you amend your order to allow Evie to reside with Dr Joanna Barratt for the weekend. She is a veterinarian in Dr Brook's practice, a close family friend and I can personally vouch for her character.'

'Get her on the phone,' sighed the judge, 'if she agrees, I will allow it.'

Joanna did more than get on the phone. She jumped on

the subway and came down to the courthouse in a little less than half an hour. The judge, keen to get to his long delayed lunch, didn't waste much time questioning her. A little later and I found myself standing with Joanna outside on the grey steps of the Courthouse, shielding my eyes from the garish sun. A shadow approached me and reached out a hand as if to touch my shoulder. I shrank away.

'Don't you dare touch me,' I shrieked, 'this is all your fault. I HATE YOU. I WISH YOU WERE DEAD! YOU'RE THE ONE THAT SHOULD BE DEAD, NOT MUM!'

Mr Tully pulled Michael away and as the sun slid behind a white puffy cloud, I caught a glimpse of the haunted stricken look on his face. I didn't care.

# Chapter 32

I watched Joanna expertly lock her apartment door – three separate locks and a long pole, one end of which fit neatly into a hole in the floor and the other slid into the middle lock. It feels just like prison, I thought gloomily. Joanna, catching sight of my face, gave an apologetic little laugh.

'Habit! When I moved into this apartment, the neighborhood was still called Hell's Kitchen and nobody had even heard of "gentrification." Anyway, make yourself at home.'

I nodded and gazed around her small apartment. It didn't take long. There was a sagging white futon, an old-fashioned, bulky TV and a solitary chair. It didn't have a kitchen, just a beaten up toaster oven. Joanna led me into the small bedroom and switched on the air conditioning unit in the window. It spluttered for a few seconds and then died. Joanna picked up a large tome, 'The Veterinary Bible,' and gave the unit a couple of hard whacks. It cranked noisily and reluctantly into operation.

'You get used to its quirky ways,' said Joanna, 'would you like to lie down on the bed before you fall down. You look so tired.'

'No, I'm ok. And no way am I taking your bed. I'll be fine on the futon.'

Joanna tried to insist that I take her room but I refused to budge and eventually she reluctantly relented. What I wanted to do was go into the bathroom and cry for a long time, maybe hours, but the apartment was so tiny, there's no way I could that without Joanna hearing me. Only a terribly rude, inconsiderate guest would throw a crying fit, I realised.

I sat on the futon and flipped on the TV, just to create some sound to try and drown the noise in my head. Sure, I'd been a little scared of losing the custody case, but I hadn't believed it would happen. Not really. Now, I felt that I would very likely be on my way to Australia with Michael before school even finished for the year. He'd probably let me visit Scott for a week or so at Christmas. For the rest of the time I would be alone. I didn't know anyone in Australia. They'd make me learn Australian English and I would start calling sunglasses 'sunnies'.

I heard Mum's voice in my head as clearly as if she were sitting on the futon beside me.

'Stop feeling sorry for yourself, Evie!'

I tried to talk to Mum in my head but she didn't say anything else.

I don't care what Michael does, he will never get me to eat kangaroo steaks, I thought defiantly.

My phone beeped – anxious text messages from Kylie and Greg.

'Are you going to answer those?' asked Joanna walking

into the room.

'Later,' I said, 'I'm too tired now.'

'Would you like me to call Kylie and Greg and let them know where you are and what's happening?' Joanna asked softly.

I nodded.

'I could invite them over to keep you company.'

I shook my head violently. 'I'm too tired,' I repeated, and I was. I felt like I could sleep for the rest of my life or at least a week.

When I woke up, it took me a couple of minutes to figure out where I was. The TV was on low, a Wonder Pets cartoon. Joanna was in the bedroom speaking quietly to someone on the phone. It was hot in the living room and the futon covering was made of some kind of scratchy material that made my legs itch. I felt an intense profound loneliness. And, I was afraid. I kept seeing Coltan's smooth blond hair and his privileged, sneering voice.

A loud buzzing reverberated through the apartment. Joanna came out of her room, spoke into the intercom and began to unlock the series of bolts. When she finally finished and flung open the door, I heard the familiar tread of snow-shoe paws and Ben jumped up on the futon beside me and licked my face enthusiastically. His tongue felt rough like sandpaper but I welcomed it all the same.

'BEN,' I called out and buried my face in his floppy ears. Attached to his collar was a note with 'EVIE' on the outside. I unfolded it.

'Evie, I'm sorting this mess out. Everything's going to be fine. Trust me. Miss you and love you. Look after Ben for me and hang in there. Scott xx

PS Don't let Joanna persuade you to try any of her cooking. Anything produced in that toaster oven of hers is lethal.'

I felt the wetness of tears of my face but I was also smiling. Joanna handed me a bag, which Scott had packed for me – some clothes and a toothbrush and my favourite framed photograph of Mum. I placed it on the floor beside the futon.

The rest of the weekend passed by incredibly slowly. I kept meaning to get up and go meet Greg and Kylie and came up with a plan. We had defeated Leela before. We could do it again but I was just so very, very tired. It was like I had some kind of sleeping sickness. My arms and legs felt like they didn't belong to me. I slept, watched a little TV, played with Ben, ate a little and then slept some more. Finally, on Sunday evening, panic set in and I forced myself off the futon.

'I have to go Joanna,' I said, 'we're back in court in the morning and I haven't fixed anything. I haven't done anything. I haven't even started to do anything, like confront Camille and Coltan and get them to back down.'

'Evie, trust in Scott. He's got it under control. Sometimes, it's harder to be the one being helped instead of doing the helping. You still look so pale and shaky. Go back to sleep. We have a big day tomorrow.'

I slept.

# Chapter 33

I stepped off the elevator on the fifth floor of the Court building. The first thing I noticed was the bustling crowd of people surging into Justice Hansen's courtroom. As I got closer, I recognised a familiar lemon shaped bald head.

'Stan,' I exclaimed, 'what are you doing here?'

Stan shifted from one leg to the other uncomfortably, looking about as out of place as possible. He fiddled uneasily with the knot in his tie as if he'd never worn a tie before. He probably hadn't. I gazed around in confusion. All the faces in the crowd were familiar: Mr Fannelli, Eurdes, Virpi, Mrs Billington, our doormen, Frank and Juan, Velda, the waitress from our local diner and lots of pet owners who regularly visited the clinic. I felt hands clapping me enthusiastically on my back as I squeezed myself into the noisy, overflowing courtroom. All of the benches were filled and more people stood packed tightly against one another, taking up every inch of standing space.

'Could you please remove your elbow from my personal space?' a familiar voice complained loudly to the tall man beside her.

I whipped my head around. Mrs Rubenstein! And the tall man was Scott's best friend, Jake.

Scott stood at the top of the courtroom, right in front of the Judge's desk, flanked by Greg and Kylie. They all waved at me.

'Make space to let Evie through,' a woman said without opening her mouth.

I whipped around.

'Sonia!' I said.

She smiled at me and gave me an awkward thumbs up sign.

I struggled through the crowd to reach Scott. He swung me up and around, as if I was a little girl but I didn't mind although we did nearly knock Mrs Rubenstein over.

'They all insisted on being here,' Scott said to me, half-laughing, 'when they heard we were in trouble, they just started turning up at the clinic and demanding to know where the judge lived!'

'All rise for the Honourable Judge Paul Hansen,' sang out the court clerk from under her desk, where she had taken refuge from the crowd.

The judge walked in, paused briefly in surprise at the size of the crowd and then proceeded to sit down at his desk.

'What's all this about?' he demanded.

Rob answered. 'Witnesses your Honour – witnesses to testify to the fact that Evie couldn't possibly have a more loving home than the one she has now.'

The crowd burst out into raucous cheering.

The Judge, banged ineffectually on his desk with the case for his glasses, but nobody could hear him over the din. Finally, he shouted,

'QUIET! THIS ISN'T A ZOO. IF I HEAR THE SOUND OF ANYONE'S VOICE BUT MY OWN, I'M THROWING YOU ALL OUT OF HERE. DO I MAKE MYSELF CLEAR?'

There was a hushed assent.

'That's better,' said the judge grumpily.

With a few well-judged jabs of his sharp elbows, Mr Tully created enough space to get to his feet.

'Your Honour,' he wheedled, 'I am requesting a continuation of the stay-away order.'

Eurdes could be clearly heard asking, 'The man, the one who looks like rat, what he say?'

'Trying to keeping Scott and Evie apart,' answered someone else.

The crowd began to chant, BOO, BOO, BOO. The Judge banged on his desk rather hopelessly with his glasses case. His face turned so purple, I thought he might be about to have a heart attack or a mini-stroke, at the very least.

When the crowd finally quieted down, the judge said, 'That's it! I can't conduct a trial in these circumstances. EVERYONE OUT except for the parties in the case and their lawyers.'

Almost everyone in the crowd seemed to take that as their cue to consult their neighbors about what the Judge meant.

Michael stood up and tried to speak, but nobody could hear him. Pushing aside Mr Tully's restraining arm, he climbed up on his chair and faced the Judge.

His voice rang out clearly.

'That won't be necessary Your Honour. I had a visit at my hotel over the weekend from a young man who helped me realise that I'm doing the wrong thing. I guess I wanted so badly to be part of my daughter's life, to try and make up for the thirteen years I wasn't there for her or her mother, that I allowed myself to be convinced that this lawsuit was the right thing to do.'

Turning his face away from the Judge, Michael looked directly at me.

'Evie, I'm sorry. This is stopping right now. All of it. I am withdrawing my petition.'

'What's the man standing on the chair saying? I can't hear a thing,' complained Mr Fannelli loudly.

'HE'S GIVING UP. WE'VE WON,' said somebody else, 'THREE CHEERS FOR EVIE AND SCOTT!'

The judge rose to his feet, 'Anyone cheering will be taken away to jail for contempt,' he said, 'and I don't advise anyone to test me on that.'

Mr Tully waved his arms in the air to attract the Judge's attention.

'Your Honour, I respectfully request an adjournment so I can speak to my client. He's clearly been intimidated by this mob! We are in a court of law!'

'Sit down, Mr Tully,' snapped the judge, 'I'm not senile. I don't need you to tell me where I am.'

'But, Judge,' whined Mr Tully in his nasally voice, 'You

cannot allow this court to be ruled by the mob!'

'Mr Tully,' said the judge, 'this is a court established by a government of the people, by the people and for the people. Who do I see before me? THE PEOPLE! That's right, the people! All through the weekend, I have been inundated with affidavits from witnesses testifying to Dr Brooks' good character. They came by email, they came by fax, they even hand delivered them to my home in the middle of the night. It will probably take my clerk a year to sort through them and file them all. And, I have to say; I've never received affidavits written in screenplay format before. That was a first.'

I glanced over at Greg and he beamed with pride.

'Thank you,' I mouthed.

The judge cleared his throat nosily.

'I am convinced that there was no improper conduct on Dr Brooks' part. As to the two young people behind the false allegations and whoever put them up to it, it will be up to Dr Brooks and Evie to decide if they wish to pursue that with the police.

Mr Tully, your client has withdrawn his petition. There is no case before me. Custody of Evangeline Carey Brooks remains with her uncle, Dr Scott Brooks. I suggest everyone leave my courtroom now before I change my mind.'

# Chapter 34

It's all over now. I can officially live with Scott forever or at least, until I go to college. Things around here are more normal than they have been in a very long time.

Scott's like he used to be, laughing and kidding around all the time, not staring unseeing into space like a zombie. Next week is the last week of school and I'll be free for the whole summer to help out in the clinic. We're going to spend two whole weeks in July at Highland Lake. Sweet. Lorcan's coming home in a few days and I'm looking forward to seeing him.

I should be the happiest, least angsty girl in the universe and I am, I am, but I'm also *not*. I don't know why. I feel a bit weird as if I haven't eaten in a whole day. I've been hiding out in my room for much of the weekend, thinking about Mum a lot. I can't find a single song that suits my mood. Every song seems faintly accusing, like I've done something wrong, not a lot wrong, but a little.

I glance at Mom's locked box sitting as always on the top shelf; waiting for the day I turn sixteen and can open it and find out what Mum has to tell me. Scott doesn't believe for a second that I haven't peeked into it. Greg and Kylie thought I should open it during the custody trial. But I didn't. I've never opened it. I'd like to think that was because I respected Mum's wishes about my waiting until I'm sixteen. But I'm not nearly that much of a decent person. I didn't open it because I didn't want to. When someone's dead, they're gone, with nothing left to say. While I have this box, a part of Mum is still alive; she still has something left to say to me. I want to hold on to that.

And, I don't need to open a box to find out what Mum would think about Michael turning up. She would say that he made a mistake and I should forgive him because he was only a scared teenager when I was born. But I'm not Mum. I'm not nearly as good a person. Oh, I can forgive Michael for abandoning me. But I can't forgive him for abandoning her.

Mum wouldn't want me to shut Michael out. I'm sure of that and I think that's why I feel bad. 'It never hurts to talk,' she used to say. I don't agree with that. Sometimes, it does hurt to talk. But not talking also hurts in a weird way.

I pull down Scott's iPad from my shelf and begin to type an email:

Hi Michael,

This is Evie. I know you're back in Australia now and I wanted to say thank you for dropping the custody case. It was really cool when you stood up on your chair the way you did. Rob told us that you had no idea about Mr Tully's plans for using Camille and Coltan to lie about Scott.

I'm sorry for saying that I wished you were dead. I didn't mean it. I was just so angry. I'm glad you're alive and I think it's really great that you are a music producer and you can sing and play the guitar. I can't sing a note and I'm not being falsely modest about that. I suppose this isn't the most appropriate time to ask you about helping my friend Kylie with becoming a celebrity, ha, ha. Seriously, that was a joke!

I saw a photograph of your wife, Emily, in the court papers. She looks nice and I bet she's glad to have you back home.

Mum would be happy that you came to find me. She always believed that you would. I think you should know that.

I'm sorry I didn't try and listen to you when you first came here, before all the court stuff happened.

If it's ok with you, maybe we could email each other now and then if you're not too busy.

Evie


I hit send before I can change my mind. I feel better, but still a little uneasy.

# Chapter 35

It came to me a few days ago, when I was in the shower trying to remember if I had already put the conditioner in my hair or not. I realised what was still bugging me. Coltan. Why had he done it? Why did he hate me so much?

Camille — that was easy. She'd never liked me and she was jealous because I was going out with Lorcan and she might even have been jealous that somebody actually bothered to try and get custody of me. Nobody was fighting for her. It wasn't hard to forgive her. I almost felt sorry for her. Being popular at school was so important to her and lots of the kids at school didn't even speak to her anymore. Scott and I decided that was punishment enough for her and we weren't going to complain to the police about her perjury. We wanted to do something about Leela's involvement, but were hampered by our lack of proof. Some West Coast publisher stepped in and took that problem off our hands by offering Leela a book contract for her silly cooking book for divorced dads.

Leela's face is now plastered on billboards all over town. Joanna heard her give an interview on the radio and she said that she was moving to LA to present some new TV show where she cooks alongside divorced celebrities. Wow, sounds fascinating. Not.

None of us could figure out what Coltan's motivation was although Greg suggested that maybe he was the one that loosened the girth on my saddle. I had an idea that Finn might know. He's pretty sharp about why people act the way they do. I went to his Dad's apartment to see him. I owed him a thank-you anyway. He hadn't been in court on the day we won, but it was pretty obvious that he was the 'young man' that stuck his nose in my business by visiting Michael at his hotel. It is super annoying to have to thank someone when you didn't want their help in the first place, so I'd been putting it off.

Finn's dad opened the door.

'Hi, Dr Winters,' I said politely, 'is Finn here?'

'Finn,' Dr Winters called out smoothly, 'the Irish girl is here to see you.'

He said it the same way you'd say, 'There's a bag of garbage at the door.'

I've met Dr Winters heaps of times and he never bothers with my name.

'Thank you, how kind,' I said in my poshest accent.

Dr Winters shot me a quizzical look. I smiled innocently back at him.

'I'm going to my home office,' he said.

Do you want my permission, I thought cheekily. But what I said was 'Ok, bye,'

Finn strolled into the hallway, looking super surprised.

'Greg's not here, Evie. He's at the Young Filmmaker's Club.'

'I know,' I said, 'I came here to see you.'

'Do you need some help with math?'

'No,' I said, 'I wanted to talk to you.'

Finn didn't look pleased. He didn't seem welcoming at all.

'It'll only take a minute,' I said, gritting my teeth.

'Ok,' he said and I followed him into the living room, which was filled with hundreds of books.

I had to take some books off a chair before I could sit down.

Finn didn't sit. He paced up and down the carpet in front of me. So rude, I thought.

'Um, I never thanked you for going over to Michael's hotel that time and persuading him to drop the case.'

'That's ok, I didn't really say much. I think Michael had pretty much already decided to stop the madness.'

'Oh,' I said.

'Don't freak out, but Michael seems like a pretty good guy,' said Finn.

'I'm not going to freak out,' I said, 'but although I'm grateful, you shouldn't have done it. You shouldn't have gone anywhere near Michael. You're not my big brother. I don't need you to sort out my life.'

'I didn't do it for *you*,' said Finn. 'I did it to keep you here in New York, not thousands of miles away in Australia.'

'Why?' I asked curiously.

There was a silence. I felt like I could close my eyes and

recall exactly every tiny detail in the room, what Finn was wearing, what I wore, the titles of the books, the colours of the pictures, Dr Winter's cherished netsuke collection carefully arranged in the glass case, the little tortoise out in front.

'I guess it's for Greg's sake because we're friends,' I said.

There was a silence again. Finn is much more comfortable with silence than I am. He didn't seem inclined to say anything. If I were Finn, I would have offered me a soda. I couldn't offer him a soda. It wasn't my apartment.

I stood up. 'Umm, one other thing. I thought you might know why Coltan lied?'

Finn looked startled. 'What makes you think I'd know what goes in Coltan's head?'

I shrugged. 'Forget it. It was just a gut feeling. See you round,' and I headed for the door.

'Wait,' he said.

I turned around.

'It was because of *me*. Coltan was like, in love with me or something.'

'What?' I said. But my mind was moving faster than my mouth. I thought of Coltan helping to look for Dr Pepper. I remembered thinking what does Coltan want from Finn. NOTHING. He didn't want anything *from* Finn. He wanted … Finn.

Finn turned slightly red.

He tried to joke. 'Are you saying I'm not good-looking enough for Coltan to be interested in?'

'I didn't know Coltan was gay,' I said matter-of-factly.

'Nor did I,' said Finn.

'So, your girlfriend's twin brother had the hots for you. That's like a bad sitcom. Oh my God, does Tamara know?'

'No, nobody knows but you, me ... and Coltan. That's the way it's going to stay. Tamara loves Coltan. She suspects that he's gay but she doesn't know that he was um, into me. I don't want her to know. It would freak her out. She—'

But I cut him off. I wasn't in the mood to hear about great Tamara is. I know that already.

'I frowned. 'So Coltan told you he liked you and I'm guessing that didn't go well. What has that got to do with me? Why would that make him hate *me*?'

I stared at Finn, who looked even more uncomfortable ... and so very distant. Unreachable. I suddenly felt sorry for Coltan. I'm not sure that anyone could really reach Finn, not Tamara, not even Greg, nobody.

Finn stared back at me. He didn't move. He just stood there watching me. Finally, he spoke, and when he did, it was in a light-hearted, jokey tone.

'Coltan was crazy jealous of you because he somehow got it into his head that I like you. Go figure.'

I stared at him. He picked up a book from the side-table and began flipping through it. 'Crazy,' he said.

Seriously, could he be more insulting, I thought.

'Crazy,' I agreed angrily. 'I wouldn't touch you with a barge pole.'

'With a what?' he asked, looking bewildered.

'A BARGE POLE ... it's an Irish expression ... obviously

from back in the day when travelling by barge was a common method of transport … just forget it. I have to go.'

This time, I really did walk through the door and out the corridor towards the front door as quickly as possible without actually running.

'Evie,' he called, coming after me.

'Don't stress it,' I called back, 'I'm not going to tell anyone about Coltan.'

'I know you won't,' he said.

'I have to go. Lorcan's back from Hong Kong. He's waiting for me.'

Finn stepped back.

'Have fun,' he said coolly.

'We will,' I snapped and I left.

# Chapter 36

I think I got Scott the best birthday present of his life. I secretly had his Harley fixed. I had lots of help, mainly from Scott's best friend, Jake, who knows a thing or two about bikes. Kylie also helped by going with me to the Diamond District so I could sell the almost-a-carat diamond earrings Mum left me – to pay for the cost of fixing the bike. When I told Kylie my plan at first, she was horrified.

'So let me see if I've got this straight?' she said slowly, 'you want to flog your dead Mom's earrings, the only jewellery she left you.'

'Correct,' I said calmly.

'And I thought *I* wasn't the sentimental type,' said Kylie.

I giggled. 'You're not! And nor was Mum – not about stuff like chips of rock that come out of the ground. She left the earrings to me to do whatever I wanted with them and I want to do something really special for Scott.'

'You have such thick hair, nobody ever sees your ears anyway,' said Kylie, 'but you can't sell them in the Diamond District, that's for tourists. You'll get a bad deal there.'

'Not if I have you with me,' I said.

Kylie's eyes gleamed. She loves to bargain.

'Okay, on one condition.'

'Name it,' I said.

'You don't open your mouth. Not one word. Leave it to me!'

I laughed. Kylie knows I'm hopeless at bargaining.

'I promise,' I said.

The Diamond District was disappointing. I thought it would resemble a jewellery fantasyland. But it was a very ordinary, fairly run-down neighborhood, a few blocks south of Radio City Music Hall. There were thousands of jewellery booths and stores. None of them were flashy. They looked more like the ninety-nine cents stores you see in strip malls in New Jersey. By the end of the day, my feet were sore from trailing Kylie from store to store as she sussed out the best possible deal, especially because Kylie had insisted that we wear high heels, oversized dark sunglasses and siren red lipstick. The pain in my feet was worth it because Scott was so overwhelmed with joy when I wheeled out his Harley that he couldn't speak.

We had his birthday brunch at our local diner. It rained all morning. Wow, when it rains in New York, it really, really rains. We had the big table close to the door and every time someone entered the diner, we all got sprayed with raindrops. Our pancakes got a bit soggy, but they get soggy with the syrup anyway. Joanna couldn't come to brunch because she had to accompany Jeffrey to some important meeting downtown in the new WTC 7 building.

After brunch, Scott's birthday guests went home and Scott and I dashed through the puddles, him holding his trench coat over both of us, which was a real sacrifice because it's his best one and he doesn't usually take it outside when it's raining. As we reached the door of the clinic, I said, 'Brunch was perfect, except of course for Joanna not being there.'

Scott stood there with rivulets of rain sliding down his face and looked at me as if I had just announced that there was peace in the Middle East. Maybe, not quite like that, maybe more like, I'd said they'd invented a banana that tasted like banana cheesecake. He ran his hands through his sopping hair, laughed manically and began to run up the block. I stared after him.

'Come on,' he yelled, 'we need to get a cab,' and I ran after him.

'Where are we going?' I yelled.

'To get Joanna of course!'

YES! I thought.

We chased every yellow cab in a six-block radius, but it's impossible to get a cab in New York when it is raining.

'Forget this, too slow,' said Scott and grabbing my hand, he half-pulled me back to the clinic. He wheeled the almost-as-good-as-new Harley out of the waiting room and handed me a helmet. We roared all the way downtown, dodging around cars and with me screaming when we went through the puddles. I'd never been on a motorbike before. It was a fantastic feeling, tinged with fear.

I have to admit some of our euphoria evaporated a little as we stood, dripping, before the security desk in the intimidating glass lobby of WTC 7. The security guard was old with grey hair and a face like a constipated Schnauzer. Scott pleaded with him to let us go up to where Joanna was at her meeting on the 49th floor, but he was immovable.

The more we begged, the more irritated he got.

'What part of no don't you guys understand?' he snapped.

I stood on my tippy toes and leaned over his desk.

'Sir, please, you know that really old movie, the one where at the end, the couple meet at the top of the Empire State Building?

'Yeah,' said the man, 'sure, the one with Cary Grant and Deborah Kerr.'

'No, with Tom Hanks and Meg Ryan, but anyway, it's a super old film, maybe they've remade it, but the point is – this is one of those moments. Scott, HAS to get upstairs or else, he might lose Joanna forever.'

The security guard snorted.

'This isn't the Empire State Building.'

He was a very practical man.

'Right,' I said, trying not to sound sarcastic, 'but don't you see, if you don't let Scott go upstairs, you'll always be the security guard that got in the way of TRUE LOVE.'

The security guard looked at me, then at Scott and back at me.

He pulled out two security badges and passed them over the counter.

'I can't believe I'm doing this,' he said with a groan, 'they'll probably have my job! I could lose my pension!'

I reached up and gave him a huge hug, which surprised me more than him because I'm not normally a touchy-feely person.

'Get out of here,' said the security guard.

When the elevator doors opened on the 49th floor, Scott ran out and I followed him. He came to complete standstill and I bumped right into him, banging my knee painfully against the helmet in his hand.

We had figured Joanna and Jeffrey were at a meeting with two or three other people but there was about fifty people in the room, all very important looking and dressed in suits, sitting around a long table. And, most surprising of all, the Mayor was sitting at the head of the table.

Everyone turned around in their chairs to stare at us. You could almost smell their disapproval. Joanna's red hair gleamed from near the bottom of the table.

'There she is,' I said to Scott, pointing, 'beside Jeffrey.'

Scott raised his hand in a casual half-wave.

'Hi, everyone, um, sorry to interrupt your meeting, and by the way, Mayor, whatever the tabloids said, you did a great job with the clean-up of the city after the snowstorms this winter.'

There was a deafening silence.

I poked Scott in his arm. He took the hint.

'Excuse me everyone, but if I could have a minute or maybe two with Joanna, I mean Dr Barratt, she's my colleague, just a quick emergency consultation, I have a Chi-huahua patient with a dangerous case of ... conjunctivitis. Um, that's one sick little puppy.'

I rolled my eyes.

Joanna stood up and hissed loudly, 'Scott, what the hell are you doing? You can't roll up here demanding to talk to me. Have you gone totally insane? I'll call you later.'

Jeffrey stood up, reaching nearly to her shoulder and said smoothly, 'Could we get some security people down the back please to escort Dr Brooks and his little sidekick out of here.'

Two of the Mayor's security detail, bulky, tough-looking men in dark suits with microphones in their ears, started to approach us.

'Whoa, hold it guys,' said Scott raising both his hands, 'I was sort of hoping for a private moment but the moment's here and it's a public one so here goes: Joanna I love you, I've loved you since the very first time you turned up at the clinic in that sad black garbage bag type thing you called a dress and I've loved you every moment since. But I was too much of an idiot to deserve you. And, um, not man enough and grown-up enough and all that, but if you could give me one chance to be with you, I'd appreciate that. I mean, more than appreciate it. Much more. I'm lost without you. Nothing is good without you.'

'Awwww,' said the handful of women at the meeting.

'I can't believe this is happening,' said Joanna.

'Scott, you're deranged!' interjected Jeffrey, 'You're the very last man in the world that Joanna would want to be with.'

'I wouldn't be so sure about that,' said Joanna, picking up her handbag and walking around the table towards us.

'Awwwwwww!' said the crowd, all of them this time, even the men. One of the tough-looking security guards pulled out a baby blue and white checkered handkerchief and blew his nose very loudly.

Scott put his arms around Joanna and they had a kiss that went on for so long, it seemed like basic good manners to look away. Jeffrey stood beside me, watching them with a stunned expression on his face. I felt a bit sorry for him.

'Um, Jeffrey, Joanna told me you guys found a whole colony of those spiders in Texas, the Braken Bat Cave Mesh-weaver thingies,' I said in an effort to make polite and distracting conversation. He stared at me with a strong look of disgust. I tried again.

'The Mayor is much better looking in real life than he is on TV, 'and taller too,' I added. This time, Jeffrey gave me a withering look of contempt. I handled it very cheerfully. Without a backward glance, he stomped off.

# Chapter 37

Kylie was an experienced junior bridesmaid but I'd never been in a wedding party before. I
almost forgot – I was a flower girl once for one of Mum's
friends when I was about three and a half years old. Apparently, I circled the reception draining the dregs from the
guests' champagne flutes and collapsed not long afterwards.
My godmother, Janet enjoys telling the story of Mum being
woken in the middle of the night by my pitiful voice croak-
ing, 'Water. Please, Mommy. Thirsty. Thirsty.'

I've always had my doubts about the authenticity of that
story. I don't remember ever calling Mum *Mommy*.

Kylie dyed her hair the same vivid shade of aquamarine
as her bridesmaid dress. She looked like a young, Asian Katy
Perry. Her mom, Rachel, the maid of honour, wore the same
dress except in a more revealing style. Poor Ben was forced
to wear an aquamarine ribbon around his neck, to which I
attached the little white satin box, containing the matching
simple rose-gold wedding bands.

Scott asked me to be his joint best man with Jake, even
though I'm a girl. I was thrilled although he wouldn't let me
go to the bachelor party.

Nikki from the tattoo parlour did my make-up and a Brazilian hairdresser friend of Eurdes's came and did my hair. Then I put on my tuxedo. I felt very grown-up with make-up and a 1940s movie star hairstyle. Rachel said that I looked about seventeen and she said that as if it was a *bad* thing. Ha!

My godmother, Janet, and her fiancée, Brendan, arrived in New York a couple of days ago for the wedding. As a super-special present for me, Scott arranged for them to bring Deirdre, my best friend from Ireland with them. Deirdre is LOVING New York and admires everything I show her. She and Kylie have not clicked at all like I thought they would. It's so disappointing when your best friends don't get along, but I'm sure they will like one another more when they get to know each other better. You see, Deirdre and I tend to talk about people and stuff we know back in Ireland and Kylie is bored. But Kylie and I talk about people we know here in New York and Deirdre gets bored. Kylie and Deirdre both love a fashion bargain. I think I just need to put them together for a day in Century 21.

Sonia at CPZ tried her best to cut through a mountain of red tape so that Scott and Joanna could get married at the zoo. But she couldn't make it happen. We were so disappointed but Greg helped me write an email to the Mayor's office. The Mayor sent a *very* nice email back and said that he absolutely remembered Scott and me. (I hope he gets re-elected. I would vote for him if I were 21). The Mayor called the clinic to let Scott and Joanna know that he, personally, had arranged for the zoo to be available for their wedding.

Joanna isn't remotely a bridezilla type; the whole wedding was organised in less than six weeks and Scott definitely agonised more about what to wear than she did.

It was Joanna who suggested that we invite Michael and his wife to the wedding. For a second, Scott looked angry and then he relaxed and said, 'That's a good idea, it's up to Evie.'

I thought about it. Michael and I had exchanged a few emails and we spoke on the phone twice. He said that receiving my first email was one of the happiest days of his life. I was glad but I didn't feel we were at the let's-hang-out-at-weddings stage and this was Scott's day, Scott's and Joanna's.

The wedding reception was held outside in the middle of the zoo on a perfect June morning with a pale blue, cloudless sky and a hint of a breeze. All of our friends and the pet visitors to the clinic attended. It was a little like the Blessing of the Animals in the Cathedral of St John the Divine except noisier. Ben, looking very dignified, trotted up the aisle beside Kylie. For one awful moment, he paused, put his nose in the air and sniffed and I was sure he was about to bolt, but after cocking his head to one side, he resumed trotting straight up to me. I untied the box with the wedding bands from around his neck and put them in my pocket. The best thing about being a best man instead of a bridesmaid is that you have useful things like pockets.

In the evening when the stars came out, the band played and everyone danced. Holly came from Chicago for the wedding and she danced with Greg five times. (He hasn't

stopped talking about it since. If Holly had more considera-
tion for those of us who are Greg's friends, she might have
danced with him a little less). A little before midnight while
I was trying not to step on Lorcan's feet, I thought about
making a wish, to freeze time, so we could all stay exactly as
we were forever. I felt the heavy weight of someone's gaze
and I looked over Lorcan's shoulder. It was Finn dancing
with Tamara and staring intensely at me. I looked back at
him.

NOBODY, NOBODY, NOBODY has eyes as darkly
beautiful as Finn's.

I didn't go ahead and make my wish. I didn't want to be
forever thirteen after all. Being fourteen could be very interesting.

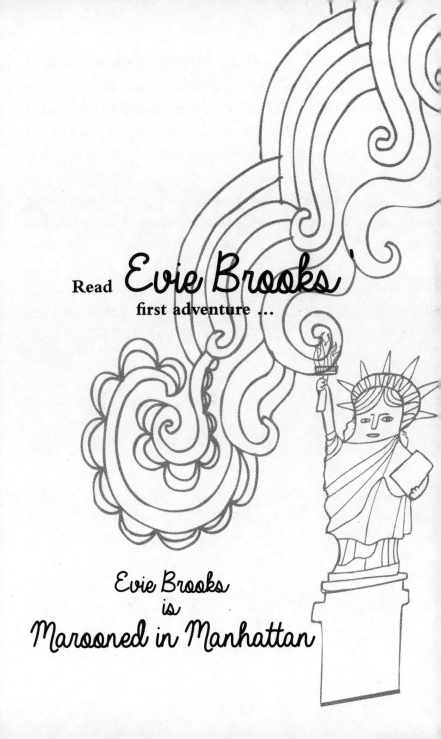

Read *Evie Brooks'* first adventure ...

*Evie Brooks is Marooned in Manhattan*

After Evie Brooks' mother dies, she is forced to go live with her uncle Scott, a vet in New York City: between the pets, their owners, Scott and his lawyer girlfriend, the summer quickly becomes a whirlwind of change and activity!